September's Fury

A Larry Macklin Mystery-Book 11

A. E. Howe

Books in the Larry Macklin Mystery Series:

November's Past
(Book 1)

December's Secrets
(Book 2)

January's Betrayal
(Book 3)

February's Regrets
(Book 4)

March's Luck
(Book 5)

April's Desires
(Book 6)

May's Danger
(Book 7)

June's Troubles
(Book 8)

July's Trials
(Book 9)

August's Heat
(Book 10)

September's Fury
(Book 11)

Copyright © 2018 A. E Howe

ISBN: 0-9997968-3-6
ISBN-13: 978-0-9997968-3-2

DEDICATION

In memory of all the storms that have affected my life, either directly or indirectly – Donna, Andrew, Frances, Katrina, Irma and Michael.

And in thanks to all the first responders who are there in the midst of the storm, and all the linemen and other folks who help to put the world back together again after the storm has passed.

CHAPTER ONE

I was sprawled on the couch with my girlfriend, Cara, binge-watching a show about a crack team of agents trying to expose a vast conspiracy. My eyelids were beginning to droop when my phone rang. Ivy, my rescue tabby, had been lying on my chest and apparently thought the conspirators were calling, springing up in terror and scratching my arm as she escaped the phone.

"That hurt!" I yelled at her as I picked up the phone and looked at the number.

"Don't tell me," Cara said, eyeing my phone as she sat up and gently removed Alvin the Pug, our other housemate, from her lap.

"You'd be wrong. It's not dispatch or any of our deputies." I was as surprised as she was. I wasn't supposed to be on call that Monday night, but it didn't always matter.

I answered the phone with a terse hello, expecting a telemarketer.

"Deputy Macklin?" said a voice that sounded vaguely familiar.

"That's right, and who are you?" I asked suspiciously.

"Hey, man! This is Luke Garner."

The image of a bearded man in a straw hat, Bermuda

shorts and a Hawaiian shirt popped into my head and I grinned. "Hey, Luke, how's it going?" I hadn't heard from him since the investigation into the murders down on Pelican Island.

"Wow, have I got something for you! Are you going to be around tomorrow? I really need to show you some stuff."

Curious what could be important enough to bring him up from the coast, I said, "Sure. How about eleven tomorrow morning?"

"Meet you at your office," he said and hung up.

"Who was that?" Cara asked from the kitchen. She'd taken the opportunity to pause the show and get a snack.

"Luke Garner, the newspaper guy from Pelican Island."

"Oh, yeah, he was nice. Do you want some cheese? Mom and Dad sent it to us."

"It's not made from armadillo milk or something, is it?" I asked.

Her hippy parents lived down in a co-op outside of Gainesville that was one step up from a commune. The culinary surprises they frequently sent usually fell into one of two categories: *Wow, that's great!* or *What the hell is this?*

"Seems to be normal and it tastes pretty good," she said, chewing thoughtfully.

"I'll take some then, along with crackers and a beer. Never mind, I'll get up." One of the house rules was that, if you asked for enough to require the other person to make a second trip, then you got up and fetched it yourself.

"What'd Luke want?" Cara asked as I reached into the fridge for my beer.

"I don't know, but he sounded excited. Of course, he always sounds excited."

"The Klein case is closed, right?"

I thought a moment before answering. The Florida Department of Law Enforcement had taken over the murder investigation after the arrest of the corrupt local sheriff, so I wasn't privy to all of the details.

"Yes and no. Since they never found Blake Klein's body,

FDLE couldn't do more than say they felt sure he had committed the crimes. Officially, though, the case is still on hold pending new evidence."

"But he *is* dead?" Cara said, bending over and giving Alvin a piece of cheese.

"There's still a wanted bulletin out for him." To keep the peace in the house, I offered Ivy a small bit of the cheese, which she licked and then rejected.

"Is it possible he survived?"

"Anything's possible, but from what Dad and I saw, I doubt it. There was some serious damage to his boat. Besides, he would have surfaced by now. Pun intended. It's not that easy to stay off the radar."

"But he was pretty clever with all his electronic gizmos."

"He was nothing more than a sophisticated Peeping Tom and a nasty blackmailer," I reassured her. "I didn't shed any tears when he died."

We settled back down on the couch.

"So did Luke give you any idea what he wants to talk about?"

"He just said he had some information to show me. We're going to meet in the morning."

"Uh oh."

"What?"

"That's what the victim always does in the movies. They say they have information on the killer then, next thing you know, they wind up with a knife in their back," Cara explained.

"I'm not too worried," I said, pulling her close to me. We watched the rest of our show and called it a night.

As I drove to the office the next morning, I passed one of several billboards that had recently been erected throughout Adams County. This particular sign bore a photo of men in striped outfits walking through a prison gate, along with the words: *A good sheriff doesn't let prisoners go free.* Small print on the billboard proclaimed that the message had been paid for by the Citizens for a Safer County PAC.

Closer to town, I saw a dozen yard signs on different street corners asking voters not to re-elect the sheriff. All of them had also been brought to us by the CfaSC PAC. I cringed at every sign I passed. They were the reason I'd been getting the silent treatment from my father for almost two weeks.

My mood didn't improve when I got to the sheriff's office and had to hunt for a parking space. Half of our lot had been taken up by a chain link fence bearing signs for the A1 Tally Construction Company. They were getting ready to start on a large addition to our building, although, near as I could tell, the preparations mostly involved fencing off a huge section of our lot to park their heavy equipment.

When I got to my desk in the criminal investigations department, I found Darlene Marks and Pete Henley already sorting through the morning reports.

"You're here early," I said to Pete. My old partner usually spent his mornings at a local restaurant, taking in coffee and gossip. While it might sound like a waste of the department's time, it allowed Pete to keep his ear to the ground and gave him a better knowledge of the undercurrents of the county than any other deputy on the force.

"Just trying to give a little extra service. Some of us actually *want* your father to get re-elected in November," Pete said with a grim smile.

"Not really funny," I said.

"No, it's not," Darlene agreed. "I saw the newest billboard. Ouch!"

"Yeah, not one of my favorites." The one she referred to had a picture of Dad and me with one word in three-foot-high letters: *Nepotism?*

"McCune's an ass," Pete said. "He might have done this even if you hadn't gone in there and metaphorically kicked sand in his face."

Horace McCune was a rich jerk who didn't like the job

my father was doing as sheriff. When Darlene and I had aggressively questioned him about a series of murders the month before, he'd gotten his shorts in a wad and decided to spend some of his cash to make sure Dad lost the election in November. As part of his plan, he had formed a PAC and blanketed the county with signs suggesting all manner of misconduct by the sheriff's office under Dad's leadership.

"I didn't do half of what I wanted to do to him," I grumbled.

"You did enough, Larry boy," Pete said in a poor Irish accent. "Stay away from him. He's golden now. Anything you do now would be seen as retaliation."

"Which is another thing that pisses me off," I said. "Now McCune has free rein to do whatever he wants."

"If it's any consolation, I saw Chief Maxwell the other day and he wasn't very happy about his new ally," Darlene said. She had worked under Charles Maxwell for several years as part of the Calhoun Police Department and had remained on good terms with him.

"I'm sure he'll be happy enough to pin on the sheriff's star if he wins," I said.

The negative yard signs and billboards had put the whole office in a solemn mood. Maxwell wasn't the worst law enforcement officer in the world, but most of the folks in the department didn't have half the respect for him that they had for my father. On top of that, everyone knew that if a new sheriff came in then there would be changes. Unlike police departments, deputies work at the pleasure of the sheriff, so a new sheriff can, and usually does, make a number of changes in staffing and leadership.

As we talked, we sorted through the reports from the night before. It had been relatively quiet and there were only seven. I got a burglary and an assault to add to my existing pile of cases. Most of them I worked alone, but I partnered up with Darlene on the more serious ones.

By the time I'd gone through my email, made a few phone calls and finished writing a report, it was time for

Luke Garner to show up. At ten past eleven, my gruesome imagination already had me wondering if Cara was right and Luke was going to be found dead, having just managed to write the initials of his killer in his own blood. But no, he was just on island time. He came walking through the door at eleven-thirty, wearing shorts and sandals and carrying an old leather briefcase that was big enough to hold a couple toasters. The owner and editor of *The Pelican Brief* looked like the quintessential beach bum, but he was a good journalist with an ear for a story and lots of contacts.

"Man, oh man, what's with all those signs and billboards? Who'd your father piss off?" were the first words out of his mouth.

I explained that the fault was mine as we walked to the small conference room.

"Bummer. Your dad is such a great sheriff. I'll run a story on him in the *Pelican*. I know we're in another county, but it can't hurt," he said helpfully.

I held open the door to the conference room and he chucked his briefcase down on the table with a thud. "You are not going to believe what I've got to show you," Luke said, pulling pictures and files from the case. "I did my research before coming to you."

"What's going on?" I asked, happy to have a distraction from work and the campaign.

Luke slid an eight-by-ten, high resolution, black-and-white photograph across the table to me. It showed a man sitting in the front seat of a car. He was slumped against the door with a plastic bag pulled over his head and taped around his neck. I winced. For some reason, suicides like this bothered me more than a bloody murder scene.

"A suicide? Where is this?" I asked.

"But is it a suicide? That's the question. Keep an open mind. The body was found in the state forest, just over the line in our county. The man died about two weeks ago." He slid a couple more pictures over to me.

In one taken from farther away, I could tell that the car

was a Ford Focus, about five years old. It was parked on a dirt road in the pine woods.

"It shouldn't be too hard to determine whether this was suicide or murder. The autopsy would most likely be definitive." Before the words were even out of my mouth, Luke was pulling out an autopsy report and setting it down with the pictures. "I assume you've looked through it. Did the victim show any signs of a struggle?"

"No. And he appeared to have taken drugs. They're still waiting on the toxicology report, but a bottle of sleeping pills was found in the car." He pointed out the bottle in one of the other pictures.

"Over-the-counter, not prescription," I observed. "I assume FDLE is looking into this since it was on state land?"

"They are." His eyes shone with excitement.

"So what's your interest in this?"

"I'm going to keep that a secret for a little bit longer. Bear with me," he said, touching the side of his nose in a mum's-the-word gesture.

I didn't like games, but because of Luke's enthusiasm and good nature, I dialed back my frustration and cut him some slack. "Okay, who's the victim?" I asked, playing along.

"Rudy Lynch. Thirty-five. He'd been living as a beach bum most of the summer. I guess I shouldn't say bum. According to his parents, he had a number of jobs that he worked pretty hard at. He just changed them up a lot."

"This was on Pelican Island?"

"That's right. His parents vacation on the island."

"History of drug and alcohol abuse?"

"Yes, though nothing unusual." I could tell this wasn't the direction he wanted me to go.

"What was his source of money?"

"Like I said, odd jobs and his parents."

"Did he have a significant other?"

"Nothing serious."

"So let me get this straight. A guy who's been drifting

from job to job, using stimulants, doesn't have a partner, comes to the end of the summer in his thirty-fifth year, drives off into the woods and kills himself with some drugs and a bag over his head. I'm sorry for the guy and his family, but this looks pretty straightforward. Of course, you and FDLE could have a bunch of info that could easily change my mind," I said congenially.

"FDLE isn't digging too deep," Luke admitted.

"But you aren't happy with the suicide angle."

"I have my reasons."

"I'm open. Give me something I can hang my hat on."

I was warming to the idea of digging into a case that wasn't in my official to-do pile. Suicides are always complicated. Some are predictable, though they still leave the families struggling with feelings of helplessness. But the ones that come like lightning out of a clear blue sky are particularly devastating. It's one thing to be on the receiving end of a blow you see coming, but something else entirely when you're blindsided.

"I've talked to the family. They say he was in good spirits," Luke said and saw my face. "I know, I know. I've covered enough suicides to know that the families are often the last to see it coming. But the Lynches don't seem like the kind of folks who have their heads in the sand when it comes to their kid. They admit he was a bit of a rogue. His dad said that every time Rudy would put the touch on him for money, it felt like Rudy was doing him a favor instead of the other way around."

"No midlife crisis?"

"His mother asked me how he could be having a midlife crisis when he'd never grown up. She confessed that it'd gotten to the point where it didn't even bother her that he didn't have a steady job."

"Did he do anything other than mooch off his parents?"

"He crewed on boats. Mostly fishing charters. I talked to one of the captains who said he'd made a standing offer to hire him on full time, but Rudy never wanted to be tied down. The captain said he was such a cheerful and nice guy that even if no one caught any fish, the boat still came back with everyone laughing."

"I'm sorry. He sounds like a real loss, but you know as well as I do that there's no good list of rules for people contemplating suicide. They can be jolly or melancholy. They can make plans for the next week or they can get all of their affairs in order. This has to come down to evidence," I said.

"The roll of tape he used was found under the driver's seat," Luke said.

"Okay. Were his fingerprints on it?"

"Yes. But—"

"Were anyone else's prints found on the roll?"

"No. But—"

"Luke, if you have an ace, now is the time to play it," I said, feeling confused about why he would feel this case was anything but what it appeared to be.

"I want you to look at all of the evidence without the… ace. I'm afraid that it'll cause you to jump to certain conclusions. I'm willing to stay in town for a day or two, if you'll just look over all the evidence carefully. Look for anything that points in another direction."

"There's only one other direction since his pants were zipped up, ruling out autoerotic asphyxiation. This is murder or suicide."

"That's exactly how I see it."

"You think it's murder and you have a clue pointing that direction, but you aren't ready to give it to me. You know, Cara jokingly said you might be murdered before you told me why you called. Just to be on the safe side, have you shared this information with anyone else?"

"Yes, I have. If I wind up dead, you should be able to ferret out the information pretty quick."

"Fair enough," I said, gathering up the autopsy report, police reports and pictures into one large pile. "One more thing. How did you get all of this? FDLE sure wouldn't give out this information for an ongoing investigation."

"I have friends in high and low places. Look, if these get out I'd be in big trouble and it would hurt some good people, so keep it close to your vest."

"No worries. No one around here is talking to me anyway."

"His parents live in Tallahassee," Luke mentioned, trying to sound innocent.

"Why'd you tell me that?"

"I thought you might want to talk with them." Luke shrugged, but his eyes told me he knew exactly what he was doing.

"Sure, I'll go see them, but it'll have to be after work. I can't devote a lot of time on the job to a case that isn't even ours." Even though I was agreeing, I didn't really want to go see Lynch's parents. Witnessing the grief of a parent was agonizing and I had to do it far too often. "And since I want to go over the files before I talk to them, it'll be tomorrow evening at the earliest."

"Sure. Hey, I know I'm blowing in here bringing you a whole bunch of work, but you got to believe me, there's a possible payoff," he promised.

I looked at him closely, trying to figure out what the trick was, but his eyes revealed nothing. "I'll call you as soon as I've had a chance to look it over," I said, ushering him toward the door.

CHAPTER TWO

I spent the rest of the day trying to clear cases and avoid my father. When I got home and tossed the files from Luke onto the dining room table, Cara raised her eyebrows.

"That's some pile of homework," she said.

"And it really *is* homework." I gave her a brief rundown of my conversation with Luke Garner without going into much detail.

"You're in luck. I'm in a good mood and will fix dinner tonight so you can get a start on the files," she said cheerily.

"You *are* in a good mood. What's up?"

"I got some great news at work," she said, obviously bursting to tell me what it was.

"You better tell me before I get lost in this case that isn't my case," I said, taking her hand.

"Dr. Barnhill has officially asked me to be the office manager. Comes with a pay raise and everything."

"Are you sure this is what you want?" I asked. I knew that working with the animals was her favorite part of her job at the small veterinary clinic. She'd even complained in the past when she'd had to fill in as the office manager.

"Yes. I didn't like just filling in, but we talked about the job and Dr. Barnhill told me I can make some changes that I

15

think will be great for the office and the animals. And I'll still be able to help out with tech work when we're short-handed. Besides, it will give me something a little more solid on my résumé." She blurted all of this out in a torrent of excitement.

A small voice inside my head wanted me to raise some concerns, but I wasn't an idiot and I told the voice to shut up and not rain on Cara's parade. Instead, I said, "Cool! If I didn't have homework, I'd tell you to forget about making dinner and we'd go out on the town to celebrate."

"Out on the town. That's funny," she said with a huge smile.

"Okay, I'll admit, Calhoun's nightlife isn't all it could be."

"Save the thought. Later in the week we can splurge and go into the great metropolis of Tallahassee."

"It's a date. And since you're the one getting the raise, you can pay," I shot back.

"Deal."

We sealed it with a kiss before I sat down to work on the files. After half an hour, I was more than willing to take a break to enjoy the pork chops and sweet potatoes Cara had fixed for dinner.

"Is it bad?" she asked.

"The pork chops are great."

"I know the food's good, you idiot. I meant the death," she said, nodding toward the files I'd pushed to one side of the table.

"Yes, it's bad in the sense that it's a tragedy. Though I still haven't come across anything that makes me doubt suicide as the cause of death," I said, feeling frustrated that Luke hadn't given me whatever mysterious additional information he had.

Cara reached over for one of the pictures from the files. I let her look at it while I took the worst ones and put them back into folders.

"Who found him?" she asked, looking at a picture of Lynch's car parked in the middle of pine trees and palmettos.

I dug out the responding officer's report. "Two women on horseback. Janice Stowe and Mary Lennart. They rode by the car the first time thinking it was someone doing his thing out in the woods. Quote, 'There's kind of an unwritten rule that you leave people alone out here.' But when they came back three hours later and the car was still there, they got curious and rode close enough to see him slumped over in the seat. Thank goodness for cell phones and GPS. They were able to get a state trooper out there in under half an hour. FDLE was on the scene in less than two hours."

"FDLE? I see why you're a little nervous about these files. How did Luke get them?"

"He was being very coy about that. Said he knows someone. Don't eat that." This was directed at Ivy, who had jumped up on the table and started to chew on the autopsy report. I shooed her with my hand, which just made her decide to attack my waggling fingers. I finally convinced her to settle in the chair next to me. "He wouldn't have had much luck getting the files if they thought this was a homicide, but I'm sure they're pretty confident with the suicide verdict. All they're waiting on is the toxicology report to close the case out."

"Kind of a rush to judgment, don't you think?" Cara said.

I shrugged. "Looking at all the evidence, I can't say they're wrong. You can take any case and beat the dead horse until you start seeing murders in every unattended death. The truth is, though, accidents and suicides happen. In this case, the method, the place, even the victim, all suggest suicide."

"So what are you going to do?"

"I'll go over everything like I promised, and I'll also talk to the parents. Hopefully after that, Luke will tell me what his mysterious evidence or hunch or whatever the hell he has is."

Cara gave me an endearingly sappy look and told me, "You are such a nice guy."

"Maybe. Or maybe I'm just glad for the distraction. I

don't know how much damage those billboards and yard signs are doing, but they're driving me crazy."

"You had no way of knowing McCune would do something like this."

"Yeah, but maybe I should have consulted with Dad before I went out to McCune's place and kicked the rabid, half-mad, batshit crazy wolverine with more money than God," I said morosely.

"You're right, you definitely need something to distract you," Cara said. "At least you can rule out accident." She was looking over the autopsy report.

"Agreed. I'm going to ask Dr. Darzi to take a look at it too. Which reminds me, I better give him a heads-up." I pulled out my phone and sent him a quick text.

In less time than it took me to set the phone down, the county coroner had texted me back: *What do you mean you want me to look at an autopsy on the DL?*

I responded with: *I think you owe me after sending that photo you snapped of the billboard along with a laughing emoji.*

Darzi: *Didn't know it was going to be a big thing. Sorry. Want your father to remain sheriff.*

Me: *This is off duty. Can I drop by your house tomorrow with report? Just need an opinion, not official verdict.*

Darzi: *Yes, yes. After nine and before eleven, please.* He included his address in Killearn, an expansive development on the north side of Tallahassee.

"Do you think he'll see something that the original pathologist didn't?" Cara asked.

"No. I'm sure," I looked at the signature, "Dr. Hayward is a fine pathologist. But I'm just running around the diamond touching all the bases."

"Wow, a sports metaphor. Where did that come from?"

"Hey, I played little league."

"Really?"

"Well, for about a year. Until Dad arrested the coach."

"What?" Cara asked, her eyebrows raised almost to the ceiling.

"Yep. I was about eight and it was toward the end of the season. We'd just pulverized a team in one of the final games of regular play and were headed to the playoffs. While all of us kids were celebrating, Dad saw the coach talking to a friend of his. Money passed from the coach to his friend and the friend palmed a very small bag of white powder to the coach. Next thing I knew, Dad had thrown the coach to the ground and was calling for backup to come grab the other guy who was headed for the parking lot."

"Wow! Pretty stupid of them to be buying and selling at the game."

"They were being pretty discreet. No one but Dad would have known what was going on. I think the coach was just planning on having a little celebration at home. He swore he'd never been high around us. I believe it, though he was always a bit of a jerk. I think that was just his nature."

"Must have been traumatizing for you," Cara said, barely hiding a smile.

"Half of me was embarrassed to see my dad down on the ground, wrestling handcuffs onto our coach in front of my friends and their parents, but the other half of me was proud as hell. Like I said, the coach could be an ass. Of course, that was the end of the playoffs. A bunch of the parents pulled their kids from the team and no one wanted us to go out of town after that. That was the worst part for me. Two years later and there were still kids from the team who blamed me and Dad for not getting to go to the playoffs."

"I'm beginning to see how alike you two are," Cara told me.

"Ouch! You're either insulting Dad or me. Not sure which."

We heard a pathetic whine and looked down to see Alvin staring up at us.

"I think someone is wanting his evening cuddle time," I said. "Let me finish up here and I'll join you both on the couch."

I watched Cara scoop the Pug up from the floor and

head into the living room, then I skimmed through the rest of the files. There simply wasn't anything surprising in any of it.

On Wednesday, Darlene and I agreed to spend most of the day working the two active cases we currently shared. One was an armed robbery that had turned into a mess because the person calling 911 was a drug dealer who'd been robbed of his dope and cash. By the time he'd realized his tactical error, it was too late and the responding deputies wound up arresting three people, including the fool who'd called them in the first place. The only person they hadn't managed to arrest was the actual robber, so finding him had been left to Darlene and me.

The other case was a he-said-she-said instance of domestic violence where each party had received injuries. Both of them might have been convinced to drop the charges, but we weren't able to offer that option due to an unrelated case from two years before. Lt. Johnson, our current supervisor in CID, had been the lead investigator on that case and had talked the couple into dropping the charges when both were found to be at fault. However, just two months later, the husband had walked into the wife's office in Tallahassee and shot her before turning the gun on himself. Ever since, Johnson had insisted that all domestic cases be pushed as far as the evidence and the State Attorney would allow.

"What do you want to tackle first?" I asked Darlene, as she drank her morning coffee and looked at the two files.

"I've already scheduled an interview with Mr. David for nine o'clock at his shop."

"You have the pictures of his wife's injuries?"

"Yeah. I thought we'd push her case against him before we questioned him about his case against her."

"Odds are in favor of him being the main offender," I said

Darlene nodded. "Probably something like seventy percent of the cases, it's the guy, twenty percent it's both, and ten percent the wife's the primary offender."

"You're making those statistics up," I said with a grin.

"Yep."

"You're about right, though."

"That's why I thought we'd interview the husband first. We push him and get a confession, maybe we can close it out."

"Nice thought. What about the three stooges and the drug deal gone bad?"

"Heh, I'd see that movie," Darlene chuckled. "We'll hit the dealer up first. He made bail. The other two were just addicts hanging around Hitdawg like flies around you-know-what."

"Hitdawg? Seriously? Is there, like, a national registry of street names?"

"If so, all the cool ones were apparently taken by the time this bottom feeder came along. But he was screwed from the get-go. His parents named him Rufus. Rufus Roberts."

"Ouch. I'm assuming you figure the two addicts aren't going to make bail so we can get to them any time."

"Exactly. And if they were too messed up to run when the deputies showed up, then they probably aren't going to be very reliable witnesses anyway."

"Agreed. We knock on Rufus's door at noon, he should still be in bed."

"According to the DDU—that's the Drug Dealer's Union—dealers aren't required to get out of bed until at least three o'clock," Darlene quipped. "He should be up, though. I called him yesterday and warned him we'd be coming."

"Nothing like spending the day with wife beaters and drug dealers," I sighed.

"I wonder if any of them will recognize you from the billboard?" Darlene said, standing up and clipping on her phone and badge.

I did the same while giving her the middle finger.

"It's laugh or cry, my friend." Darlene headed for the door and I followed her out to her car.

Meeting Neil David at his welding shop instead of bringing him into our office was part of our plan to do a good-cop/good-cop number on him. It was often more effective to catch criminals with honey instead of vinegar.

"I could go it alone and see if I can get him with a good ol' boy routine. You know, give him the we-all-do-it number," I suggested as she drove.

"He'd never believe it," Darlene said, looking me up and down. "I'd find it easier to believe that a lamb chased a wolf."

"Okay, okay. I admit I don't have the blue collar, tough-guy thing down."

"It's okay, rover. You're just tough enough."

"I'll take that as a compliment."

Darlene parked in front of a small strip mall on the south side of the tracks. David's shop took up two storefronts at the end of the mall. I'd never been over to his place, but I'd already pictured it in my head as a stereotypical greasy, dirty workshop. While the bays where his employees were working fit that description, the waiting room and office space took me by surprise. I'd seen waiting rooms in health clinics that weren't as clean.

David must have been looking out for us because he met us at the door and quickly ushered us into his office. He was completely average looking—from top to bottom, there was nothing north or south of the norm about him. He was wearing a clean white work shirt bearing a badge that read: "Neil, Owner, David's Metal and Welding."

"Hey, come on in. Can I get you something? Coffee? Tea?"

"We're fine, Mr. David. You know this isn't a social visit?" Darlene said.

"Have a seat." He pointed to the two leather chairs facing his neat oak desk. "Yes, I understand. I spoke to my lawyer. He said I shouldn't talk with you. Of course, that's just because he wants me to refer you to him so he can bill me for fifteen minutes every time he sends you an email or answers a phone call."

"Business seems to be doing well," I said, looking around the office.

"We do all right. Honestly, most guys that are any good with their hands can make a decent living. Hell, even a great living. What screws them up is their failure to manage their finances. I run a tight ship." David gave a self-deprecating laugh. "Listen to me. I sound like my dad."

I opened a folder I'd brought with me that contained pictures of the bruises and lacerations on his wife. None of them had been life threatening, but, to be honest, she looked like what you'd expect from someone who'd fallen off the back of a truck. I leaned forward and placed them on his desk.

"This is the damage you caused to your wife this past weekend."

He picked up the pictures and looked at them very carefully.

"There's nothing I can say. I have excuses, that's all. I was drunk. And she was as engaged in the fight as I was. I can't even tell you who made the first physical contact."

"She says it was you," Darlene said, her tone even and non-accusatory.

David shrugged. "That's possible. But I'll say that she was as drunk as I was."

"How often do you get drunk and get into fights?" I asked.

"We've been married ten years. Lately, I've seen her drink more, and she isn't keeping the house as clean or the family checkbook balanced."

"And that makes you mad." I was thinking that anyone who liked to keep his office as orderly as Neil David did probably had a low tolerance for sloppiness in others.

"I find it irritating, but that wasn't the point I was making. I think she's unhappy. More often now, she finds reasons to contradict me or to change the way we've been doing things." He was doing a good job of sounding reasonable.

"You didn't answer my question. How often do you all get into fights?"

David looked up at the ceiling as though trying to decide whether he wanted to tell me the truth or not.

"Almost every weekend," he finally answered. "The drinking for her starts on Friday. I come in here on Saturday morning, so my drinking doesn't start until Saturday afternoon. But by nine o'clock, we're both drunk and the fight is well under way. But this is the first time it's gotten physical."

"Why was this time different?" Darlene asked.

"I think it's just a natural progression. The fights have become more and more nasty. This time, she started cutting up my yearbooks."

"So you were pissed off. You grabbed her? Maybe reached for the books and knocked her over?"

"Or all of the above," he said. "After that, we ended up wrestling around the house. It just seemed that, once we'd crossed that line, the emotions poured out of both of us. I know I was saying things I knew were cruel and meant to hurt her. She was just as bitchy to me and then some."

Neil David sounded sincere and remorseful. Maybe he was, but I couldn't help wondering what would happen when he drank again and Mr. Hyde came home to roost.

"You moved out?" Darlene asked.

The judge had granted bail for both of them on the condition that he move out and they didn't contact each other directly. The court's order was valid until a decision was made by the State Attorney, guided by our recommendation on how to prosecute them.

"That's right. I'm camping out at the Road's Best Motel."

"After reading the report and hearing what you have to say, I have a suggestion," I said. Darlene looked at me, as much in the dark as David was. "I think you need to write out a statement accepting responsibility for your part of the fight."

He looked at me with narrowed eyes. "And how would that help me?"

"We aren't here to help you. I think we made that clear from the beginning," I said, and caught a quizzical look from Darlene. I was venturing far off of the good-cop/good-cop script.

"I'm fine with a misdemeanor for whatever. I've already made up my mind that we're getting a divorce. Personally, I'm going to quit drinking. That's what I can give you. I don't care what you do as far as Cindy is concerned. I don't have a grudge against her. It's my fault for not waking up and seeing the light before it went this far."

"You're getting a divorce?" Darlene asked.

"I have no desire to be with someone who obviously doesn't want to be with me. I've already told my lawyer to draw up the papers. I also told him to be fair with the settlement. Fair, not anything more."

His answer surprised me and I decided the guy might be all right. Not someone I'd want to hang out with, but someone that I'd be willing to do business with. I looked over at Darlene, who shrugged her shoulders.

"We can go with a simple assault charge. That's a misdemeanor."

"Fine. I'll tell my lawyer to expect a call from the State Attorney." David opened a desk drawer and handed me a card. "That's my lawyer."

We thanked him and left.

"Now that's how all of our business should be conducted," Darlene said with a contented smile. "All civilized with none of the usual ugliness or accusations."

"And no chasing or handcuffing."

"Let's say we grab a refined lunch and then go pay a social call on Mr. Hitdawg. Where would you like to eat, kind sir?"

"I can't do the Palmetto," I said apologetically.

"I understand. Too many eyes watching for Mr. Billboard. I guess it will have to be the taco stand. Not quite what I'd hoped for, but it'll do."

CHAPTER THREE

Taco baskets and drinks in hand, we sat down at a picnic table in the shade of a live oak. After a couple of bites, we both pulled out our phones. I texted Pete and told him where we were while Darlene browsed the web.

Still looking down at her phone, she asked, "Do you think Marcy is going to come here?"

I choked on my taco and my mind literally froze. The mere idea that my looney ex-girlfriend would show back up in town was enough to make me want to dig a hole, crawl in and pull the dirt back in on top of me.

"What on earth would make you ask that?" I said, still half choking on the taco shell.

Darlene looked puzzled, then her face broke into a wide grin. "Oh, that's hilarious! You thought I meant your Marcy. No, I meant the tropical storm that's down near Cuba."

"She's *not* my Marcy. And she *is* a tropical storm. You remember the last time she was in town."

"Good times," Darlene said with a wicked smile. "Seriously, though, they're projecting that it will enter the Gulf. This is like the fifth storm this year to do that."

"What I hate is that the hurricane center's projections are usually so far out that whenever a storm enters the Gulf, almost everyone from Florida to Texas is in the projected cone at some point."

"Sooner or later, we're bound to get another one," Darlene said with more than a bit of fatalism. She wasn't wrong. While there was a lot to love about the Florida panhandle, hurricane season frequently made it feel like we were living at the end of a bowling alley, just waiting for the next strike.

"Enough about Marcy. *Both* Marcys. How are you and your beau getting along?" I asked, referring to her new relationship with one of the county's EMTs.

"Sizzling hot, honey," she answered with an unnerving wink.

"Careful, don't drift into the TMI zone."

"Now is that fair? If I was a guy with a hot new girlfriend, you'd want all the dirty details."

"No, I wouldn't," I said flatly. "I'm the kind of guy who likes to do the deed, not hear about it."

"Now who's heading for the TMI zone?"

At that moment, a car pulled into the lot and Pete hauled his three-hundred-pound bulk out of the driver's seat.

"What's up, compadres?" he said cheerily as he passed us on the way to the taco trailer. He was back almost instantly.

"How'd you get your food so fast?" I asked. I hadn't even seen him place the order.

Pete held out his phone. "I texted ahead."

"Hell of a world we live in," I mumbled. Even though I was more than a decade younger than Pete, I was definitely on the slower end of the bell curve when it came to some forms of technology. "What kind of trouble have you been up to?"

"We might be converging on the same bad guy. You all have that dumbass who called us 'cause he'd been robbed, right?"

"Hitdawg the Mensa candidate?" Darlene said.

"That's the man. Apparently, he thinks he's on the job. He's been doing some investigating of his own trying to find out who robbed him."

"That's pretty rude of him to call us and then not give us a chance to do our jobs," I said.

"His technique still needs work. He slapped around a couple of working girls that live down in the Ditch with him, trying to question them about the robbery."

The Ditch was a low area on the east side of Rollins Creek where some genius developer had built about twenty houses back in the early sixties. Every five years or so we'd have enough rain to flood the houses. They were all small, concrete block affairs that had been built as starter homes. Now all but a few were owned by absentee landlords who used the properties to secure their credentials as official slumlords. On almost any given night, most of the houses had some form of illegal activity going on inside them.

"We're heading over that way after lunch. You're welcome to come to the party," I offered.

"Sounds like it could be fun. I'll park on the west side of the creek in case our friend decides to exit out the back."

The creek was only deep after a rainstorm. At any other time, there were usually a couple makeshift bridges of old boards or cinderblocks stretching across it to aid in foot traffic for the illicit businesses and to provide alternative escape routes when the authorities rolled up.

"You probably want to save that last taco in case you have to chase him," Darlene said to Pete. She teased everyone about everything.

"No way. If I have to run, I'll need the extra energy," Pete responded, squirting some taco sauce on the item in question. Pete got the you-need-to-lose-weight speech from the doctor every year at his physical, but it wasn't wise to underestimate his sprinting abilities. More than one bad guy had tried to outrun him and had ended up on the ground with a bear's weight of deputy on top of him.

Pete frowned at his phone, reading a text from his daughter as he took the last bite of his taco.

"How are the kids?" I asked.

He looked up, rolling his eyes. "Don't ask. New school year. Kim's not so bad, but with Jenny there's always drama. Especially now that she's a senior." Pete was one of the most involved parents I knew. The focus on his family helped him handle the darker aspects of our job.

"You ever dealt with Mr. Hitdawg before?" I asked him.

"No. These dealers come and go so fast that it's not easy to keep up with them."

"That's what they ought to tell some of these kids in middle school. Think you want to be a dealer and flash all that cash around? Fine. Just remember that your life expectancy is about twenty-five," I said.

"Got that right. I'm not sure I've ever met a street-level dealer who was older than thirty," Darlene agreed.

"I talked to Julio. He was one of the deputies responding to Hitdawg's robbery call," I said, referring to Julio Ortiz, one of the most dependable members of our department. "He's just what you'd expect. Not very bright. Shocked when Julio started asking questions about the money that the robber had taken. Even more shocked when Julio saw evidence of drug use on the premises and got a search warrant."

"Idiot," Pete said.

"Unfortunately, he's an idiot with a lawyer now. I had to do some convincing to get him to talk with us," Darlene said. "Told him that we would focus on the robber, and that he owed this guy not just for the robbery, but also for his getting arrested. Once he agreed to meet us at his house, I reminded him to clean the place up beforehand so that we wouldn't see evidence of drug use. It was like talking to a thirteen-year-old."

Fifteen minutes later we were rolling in the direction of the Ditch. Darlene had a thoughtful look on her face as she drove.

"You don't mind that Pete's coming along?" I asked her, making us sound more like a married couple than LEO partners.

"No, the more the merrier. I was just wondering how to approach it. It's always weird when you get one of these guys and he's a witness, a victim and a perp all rolled into one."

"We'll let Pete play bad cop. We need to focus on finding the guy who robbed this idiot. Because sooner or later he's going to stick a gun in someone's face and the bullets are going to fly, leaving us with a toe-tagged victim instead of a live one."

"You got that right, buttercup. We chase him now or later. Less paperwork if we catch him before there are bodies involved."

I tested my radio as we pulled up to the curb above the Ditch and Pete responded that he was in position. The road sat about twenty feet higher than the houses in the Ditch, which was another reason they were so popular as bad-guy hangouts. A cop passing by on the road couldn't see into the yards or houses. Of course, the criminal element, not being especially bright, didn't understand that the reverse was also true. They had no warning when a cop parked in the street above them.

We got out of the car and walked down the cinderblock-and-dirt path that led from the road to the front door of a ratty brown house. Old lawn chairs and other bits of trash were scattered in a yard that was filled with weeds, overgrown bushes and sweetgum trees.

Before we reached the door, it opened and Hitdawg came out onto the small concrete stoop. "Hey," he said.

"Rufus Roberts?" I asked, though he was easy enough to recognize by the rattlesnake tattoo running down his arm.

The use of his real name caused his eyes to soften for a moment and he looked down at the ground. "Yeah," he said in a sulky tone.

"We appreciate you agreeing to meet with us. Like Deputy Marks told you, we're focused on catching the man that robbed you. Your arrest doesn't concern us."

"Can we come in?" Darlene asked.

"Nah, we can sit out here," Roberts said, nodding toward

a mismatched assortment of lawn chairs set up around a charred circle of rocks.

"That'll work. There's another deputy with us who's here to talk to you about a problem you had with some of your neighbors," she told him.

"I ain't got no problem with nobody," he said belligerently.

"Regardless, he's going to sit in on our interview and, afterward, you can decide whether to talk to him or not."

"My lawyer said not to talk to none of y'all," Roberts said, putting his chin up and glaring at us.

"But you're smart enough to know that it's better if we catch the guy who robbed you. Because if something happens to him before he's arrested, you're going to be the main suspect."

"I don't even know who this bastard is. If I did, I'd've capped him already." He pointed his hand like a gun and made a shooting gesture.

"Honey, I don't normally give the other side advice, but making threats against someone in front of a couple of sheriff's investigators isn't a good idea," Darlene said, then added, "Your mother or grandmother would box your ears for that."

"Raised by my mother," he said with pride. "She didn't do nothin' wrong neither. I just screwed up."

I knew he was only twenty and, for just a moment, I could see what he'd have looked like if he hadn't spent the last four years living the drug-dealer dream life, including a combined two years in prison for different convictions. Sighing to myself, I keyed my radio and told Pete to come on around.

"I don't want to talk to no police about nothin' those skanks said."

"Mr. Roberts, that will be entirely up to you. Again, we're just here to ask you questions about the robbery," I said. He eyed me suspiciously, but didn't get up or say anything else as Pete came into the yard.

I let Darlene handle the introductions and she got his permission to record our part of the interview. "Now tell us what happened the other night," she said, after recording his name and vitals for the record.

"I already told the other cops. Two of my deal... friends had just left and, next thing I knew, this asshole was sticking his gun in my face."

"We need more details. Where were you? This was Saturday night, right?"

"That's right. I was sitting here around the fire. Two of my guys come down, we talked for a couple minutes, they leave and, bam, there's this freak in a mask pointing a gun in my face and telling me to hand over all my money and... stuff." His face showed a mixture of fury and shame at the memory of being helpless in the face of a masked gunman.

"Okay, so a couple of your dealers came by and gave you money, then after they left a man in a mask robbed you," I recapped.

"I didn't say nothin' about dealers."

"Your objection is noted. We'll just say a couple of guys who owed you money came by and repaid you. Now, exactly how long was it before the gunman showed up?"

"Five, maybe ten minutes. No more." His brows were furrowed as he tried to remember.

"Which direction did he come from?"

"I... I don't know exactly."

"Okay, is that the seat you were in?" I asked. He was in a wooden chair with armrests, the largest and most comfortable looking seat around the makeshift fire pit.

"Yeah, man, this is my chair. I catch someone sittin' in it, I box their damn ears," he said, swinging his arm so we'd know how serious he was about defending his seat.

"Was it facing toward the path from the street like it is now?"

"Hell yeah. How else you think I see the... people coming up to my house?"

"Where was he standing?"

"I guess there," Roberts said, and pointed to the chair to his left where Pete was currently sitting, watching our exchange with a slightly amused expression on his face.

"He just appeared there? You didn't have any warning? Didn't hear anything?" Darlene asked.

"No, nothin'. Bam! There he was."

We went on like this for a while until we had as full a description of the man and his movements as we were going to get. Roberts did mention that the man obviously hadn't known about the stash of money that he kept in an old coffee can just inside the house, as he'd never tried to enter the building.

"So you have no idea who this guy could be?" Darlene asked. Normally, with dealer-on-dealer crime, the victim has no trouble identifying the perpetrator.

Roberts shook his head.

"Do you think one of your dealers set you up?" I asked.

"Why you keep talkin' about dealers?"

"Okay, okay. Your friends who owed you money," I played along.

"Hell no! First thing I did was find them and slapped them around. But they ain't got the balls for doin' that."

I felt a chill settle over me. "Mr. Roberts, let me be clear. I know that a lot of people use underage street dealers. If I find out that you were slapping kids around, we'll be back for you. I guarantee it."

Darlene and Pete were both leaning forward, giving him the eye along with me.

"Nah, man, I don't use kids. That's a punk-ass move." His denial sounded pretty convincing.

"Okay, then, I think we're done for now. We'll let you talk with Deputy Henley."

"No way!" he said, standing up with his arms raised and giving Pete his warrior face. "I didn't do nothin' to those whores. 'Sides, it's their word against mine."

With a wry smile on his face, Pete pulled out his phone, tapped it and turned the screen toward Roberts. We could hear a woman screaming and Roberts yelling at her. Then there was the distinct sound of flesh slapping flesh as a woman screamed out for Dawg to stop hitting her.

Roberts's face drooped and he slumped back down in his chair. "Fuck me."

"Social media. Whatcha gonna do?" Pete said, shaking his head. "Look, Mr. Hitdawg, I don't want to go through a lot of paperwork and effort here. I'm going to arrest you and book you into jail. You call your lawyer and you can be back out again as soon as the judge assigns you bail and you pay it. That's if, and it's a big if, I don't go in there and remind the judge how you're already out on bail for one crime, blah, blah and blah. 'Cause, honestly, if he's reminded of those facts then you'll be sitting in jail until all of these cases go to trial."

By this point, Roberts was sitting with his head in his hands. After a moment, he looked back at us and said quietly, "You know where I got that nickname? I was a lineman on the Adams County High football team. I was good. Damn good. The Hit Man, that's what Coach called me. The other guys on the team would yell out, 'Hit dawg!' whenever I made a tackle. Five years ago I was thinkin' about playin' college ball. Then my back started to kill me. Hurt so bad… They told me I'd fractured something liftin' weights. I was supposed to get all of this brace and shit to wear. But my momma didn't have money for any of that. So I was off the team. I got to takin' Oxy when I could get it. Needed money so got into sellin' to pay for it. Life's a joke, man."

Without another word, he stood up and put his hands behind his back. After Pete had read him his rights, cuffed and searched him, Roberts looked at Darlene and me. "Get that son of a bitch that stuck a gun in my face."

I nodded.

"Not much to go on," Darlene said as we walked up to her car.

"No. The guy was covered head to foot. Didn't talk

much. Seemed to know what he was after."

"Though he didn't know about Hitdawg's stash inside," Darlene reminded me.

"Which means it's probably not someone with inside information. Though he could have just forgotten about it in the adrenaline rush of the stick-up."

"If Hitdawg ran a regular business, then we could check all the laid-off or fired employees. Not really an option in this case."

"I'll check with Eddie and see if there's any word on the street about other dealers being hit. Everyone might not be dumb enough to call 911 when their micro drug empire is hit."

"How's Eddie doing?" Darlene asked.

Eddie Thompson was a confidential informant that had helped me out on several cases. He was a bit of a nutcase and was a recovering drug addict, but he usually did the right thing if given enough time.

"He's okay. As of a couple weeks ago, he was still on the wagon."

"The way Albert talks about him, you'd think he was his son."

Albert Griffin, the unofficial historian of Adams County, had taken Eddie in when he'd needed a place to lie low earlier that summer.

"They have an interesting bond," I said. "I think Mr. Griffin needed someone to look after, and Eddie certainly needed a good influence after growing up with a father and grandfather that are squarely on the monster spectrum." Eddie's family had run a major drug operation in the county and had never hesitated to commit murder when they deemed it necessary.

Back at the office, we both wrote up reports and then called it a day. I managed to escape without running into Dad. Right after the last series of billboards and a flurry of yard signs had appeared, he'd told me how gratifying it was going to be when I was right behind him in the unemployment line come January. He hadn't spoken to me since and I'd gotten good at avoiding him.

CHAPTER FOUR

I went home to get a shower and change before heading into Tallahassee. Now that it was September, the air was dryer and the temperatures a little bit lower, but I'd still worked up a sweat during our outdoor interview with Hitdawg. I wanted to be fresh for visiting Rudy Lynch's parents and talking to Dr. Darzi.

Cara wasn't home yet, so I texted to let her know I'd be out late.

Her: *It'll be just awful having the evening to myself.*

Me: *I detect some sarcasm.*

Her response was an emoji with a big grin.

The Lynches lived in an old neighborhood on Tallahassee's northwest side. The house and yard were immaculate. I walked up to the porch and took a deep breath before pushing the doorbell.

The door was opened by a short, older man with grey hair that was longer than most men his age. Mr. Lynch shook my hand and ushered me inside. "Call me Martin. Come in and meet Lori," he said.

Despite the home's almost sterile exterior, the den had a comfortable, lived-in feel with books and magazines lying around on overstuffed furniture. Lori Lynch sat on a large sectional, her eyes, face and posture all speaking of intense grief. Martin joined her on the couch. They made an odd pair. She was tall and he was short. Her hair was cut short while his was a bit long. Both were dressed very casually. They grasped each other's hands and leaned in so that their sides were touching.

A lot of marriages don't survive the death of a child. The pain is so deep that the parents can barely hold themselves together, let alone their spouse or the ties that bind them. But I had seen a few couples that drew together and became stronger after a tragedy. It gave me hope to see this couple with their hands clasped.

"Thank you for meeting with me. But I want to make it clear that I'm not actually working on your son's case."

"We know. Luke said that he was going to talk to you," Martin said.

"Even if I find something that points in a particular direction, I can't guarantee FDLE will act on it."

"We understand. We," he turned to look at his wife for reassurance, "just want to know what happened. Really, it's just as unbelievable that someone might have killed him as that he killed himself."

"Deputy Macklin, you never met Rudy. He wasn't like most people and I sometimes think it was our fault," Lori said.

Martin patted her hand. "You don't mean that. He was a good man and we did a fine job raising him." Martin turned to me. "I think what she's trying to say is that, by most standards, Rudy wasn't doing much with his life. But we didn't care that he wasn't making a bunch of money or married or whatever people usually expect of their children. We taught him from day one to enjoy life and do good."

Lori nodded. "And he did. I don't think he hardly ever had a day when he was unhappy or did something that he regretted." She must have seen the look on my face because she quickly added, "I know that sounds strange. Everyone has bad days, but Rudy was so… resilient. He had a girlfriend for several years when he was in his twenties and, when it was over, they stayed amazing friends. He ended up being the best man at her wedding. The only thing that ever upset him was seeing someone harm a person or an animal."

"I was worried a few times when he tried to help people get out of abusive relationships," Martin said, causing my ears to perk up. Interfering in a domestic dispute was one way to find yourself dead. But as soon as I had the thought, I had to remind myself that I wasn't even close to being convinced he'd been murdered.

"Don't think I'm judging him with my next question, but I need to know. Did Rudy ever abuse drugs or alcohol?" I asked.

"Abuse? Do you mean was he an addict?" Lori asked.

"I mean did he get drunk or high often? I don't think a person has to be an addict to get in trouble with drugs."

"Rudy partied on the weekends with his friends. He loved the beach and its atmosphere, including the girls and the parties. But he drank to be sociable, not to get high. And he might have smoked a little weed. Look, I know what this sounds like," Lori said. "But he didn't always party. He almost always found work during the week."

"What kind of work did he do?"

Martin smiled. "That's kind of funny. Rudy was of two minds. Sometimes he liked hard physical labor like crewing a fishing boat, but he also liked being around artists. I think he tried every type of art there was, including music, painting, writing and woodwork, but he just wasn't any good at any of it. Unlike many people, he knew his limitations. At some point, he just gave up trying to be an artist himself and was content to work for artists. For a couple years, he worked for a guy who did amazing wood sculptures. Rudy started helping him out around the shop and, after a month or so, he was going on buying trips. He'd go all over the southeast, finding and purchasing these huge logs that the guy used for his sculptures. What was his name?" he asked Lori.

"Silvanus. He still has a shop down in Panama City. He

and Rudy remained good friends."

"Why'd he quit?"

"He was too good at it," Martin said. "At one point, Silvanus told Rudy that he had to stop because he'd brought him so much wood it would be enough to last for the rest of his life. He'd have kept Rudy on to help out at the shop, but by that time Rudy was looking for something new."

"That was my fault too. When Rudy was a child, I wanted him to have this enormous curiosity for life. I think it made him restless," Lori said sadly.

"It made him a fun and interesting young man who loved life," Martin reassured her, bringing her hand to his lips for a light kiss.

"Was he working somewhere when he died?"

The Lynches looked at each other and I could see the tears in both their eyes.

"That's the saddest thing," Martin said. "He was working for a woman, a musician. They started going out together and… I think it had gotten pretty serious."

"She's a wonderful person," Lori added.

"What work did he do for her?"

"She has a lot of instruments. Plays the harp, the cello and I don't know what all. Rudy helped her move her equipment from concert to concert. He also helped out with CD sales and all of that."

"And security too," Martin said. "At the end of a concert, while she was signing autographs, she needed someone to make sure her instruments were secure. Right before she hired Rudy, someone had stolen a very valuable guitar."

"But they'd started a relationship?"

"That's right. She came to dinner a few months ago when we celebrated Rudy's birthday. They made a nice couple. This was the first serious girlfriend he'd had in years," Lori said.

"Is there any chance the relationship was in trouble?"

"She called us as soon she heard and was devastated. She tried to play at his funeral, but couldn't do it. I felt horrible for her," Martin said.

"But their relationship was on solid ground?" I asked again. He hadn't really answered the question.

"She did say they had talked about their relationship a week or so before he died," Lori said.

I waited and they looked at each other.

"She told him that she didn't see it as a long-term situation," Martin finally said.

"But she didn't want to break up," Lori added hurriedly. "She just wasn't as serious as he was about it."

"What's her name?"

"Khess Fields. You may have heard of her. She's pretty well known around here for her one-woman concerts," Mr. Lynch said and gave me her phone number.

We spent a few more minutes talking about what they could expect from FDLE's investigation. I assured them the agents would be very professional, but that they weren't given to looking down rabbit holes. They just didn't have the time. Besides, most rabbit holes just held rabbits, not answers.

After leaving the Lynches, I drove across town to meet with Dr. Darzi. His house had considerable curb appeal. The large Colonial was set back one hundred feet from the road and towered over a manicured lawn that had been professionally landscaped. I parked in the driveway and walked up to the front door feeling small and insignificant in the face of this edifice to success.

When I rang the doorbell I heard yelling and laughter from the hallway on the other side of the door. A chubby, smiling face peeked out from behind the curtain of one of the windows that flanked the door. "I think it's that guy you're waiting for!" the child yelled.

A minute later, I heard the deadbolt flip and the door was opened by a stunningly beautiful woman who gave me an ear-to-ear smile.

"I'm Deputy Larry Macklin," I stuttered, wondering if I'd gotten the right house.

"Oh, yes, come in. My husband is waiting for you. I'm Riya."

I walked into a large entrance foyer with high ceilings and a winding staircase. The boy I'd seen peering out at me was standing behind his mother, while a girl who looked a little older stuck her head out of a room on the left.

Riya saw me looking at the children. "This monster is Alexander and the one over there is Marta."

"I'm not a monster," the boy said with a huge smile on his face, then he went running off toward the back of the house. We followed him and found him in a cozy office, climbing on top of Dr. Darzi as he tried to get up off of the couch.

"Where did such an unruly child as you come from?" Darzi asked, tickling Alexander as he tossed him down on the couch while making his escape. "Macklin, ignore these children. I have no idea who is responsible for them. I swear I have never seen them before."

"Tough life you have," I said, after he'd shown his wife and kids out of the room and shut the door.

"I am a very, very lucky man. What could be more perfect? I cut up corpses all day, then get to come home to a gorgeous wife and a loving family." He gave me a crooked grin.

"Me, I could do without the corpses," I said.

"A corpse is the page on which a person's life has been written. What animated the person has gone to a different place, but the body they leave behind tells a story. And unlike the person when they were alive, it doesn't lie. People try to make their bodies lie. They'll burn off a tattoo here, or nip and tuck there, which just tells me more about who they were."

"You aren't as philosophical at the office."

Darzi shrugged. "I look up from my scalpel now and then. Okay, what have you got?" He held out his hand for the envelope I was carrying.

"I'm just going to tell you the basics. What I'm looking

for is anything out of the ordinary," I said, then filled him in on where, when and how the body was discovered.

Darzi went over to a spacious oak desk and spread out the autopsy and the accompanying pictures. As he studied the report, I walked around the room and scanned the many bookshelves. As expected, medical books covered one whole wall, while another was full of photo albums, yearbooks, awards and diplomas. The surprise came when I reached the corner of the room where two large bookcases surrounded an overstuffed chair. Those shelves, floor to ceiling, contained all the classics of science fiction, everything from H.G. Wells to Samuel Delaney. There were even two shelves full of 1950s space operas. I looked over at Darzi with raised eyebrows and saw him flipping back and forth between the pictures and the report.

"No lab results yet," he observed.

"Still at least a month away."

"They were a little sloppy with the body. They didn't take a temperature until almost three hours after the body was found. Ambient temperature, where is it? Ah, here…" He grabbed a pad and pencil to do some calculations and I went back to scanning his book collection.

"One thing," Darzi finally said. I turned and saw a gleam in his eye. "I'm going to toss you a bone. A very, very small bone."

"I'm not sure I want one. One part of me wants to tell Luke that this is just a suicide and be done with it."

"Maybe it is. But if he took pills like the presence of the bottle suggests, then where are they?"

I didn't know what he was talking about. "He swallowed them," I said like it was obvious.

"You are too squeamish. Look at the picture of the vomit that was found on the inside of the bag and in his throat." He held out one of the glossy photos. Reluctantly, I took it from him and looked at it. "See, there should be remains of undigested capsules."

I looked harder at the photos. He was right.

"They aren't listed in the stomach contents either," Darzi said. He held up a finger. "But before you do your jumping to conclusions, it's possible that he crushed them up and swallowed them. Possibly in a liquid. I've seen women do that." He looked down at his desk and seemed lost in thought. "I'm not sure I've ever seen a man who committed suicide pulverize the capsules before ingesting them, but I'm sure it wouldn't be a first."

"Of course, if you wanted to give them to someone else without them knowing it, then you would crush them and put them in their food or drink."

"Exactly. Which would point to murder. But we are assuming that he took them at all. A half empty, opened bottle is the only evidence. However, your victim may have thought about it and then changed his mind. You need to get the toxicology report."

"It all takes time."

"As I tell you all the time," he chided me, neatly reorganizing the pictures and the report into the envelope. "Ninety-eight percent of the evidence seems to point to suicide. Without other evidence, perhaps something in the toxicology or at the crime scene, I would put suicide on the report." He handed me the envelope.

"You wouldn't say it was undetermined?" I asked, pushing him for as definitive an answer as was possible at this stage.

"No, and you know better than to ask. Sometimes it's impossible to be one hundred percent. With the evidence here, I would put suicide," he emphasized again.

Darzi walked me out of his office and I apologized to Riya for disturbing them at home. She shook her head and told me how much she'd enjoyed meeting me. His kids followed me to the door and waved goodbye as I drove away from the house.

On the way home, I reviewed my conversations with Darzi and the Lynches and wondered what I'd found out. Not much, was my conclusion. I called Luke Garner and told him so.

"I didn't think you would. I'll come by your office in the morning and show you what put me onto this case. It's going to blow your mind," Luke said with his usual exuberance.

The paranoid part of my brain remembered what Cara had said about the victims in movies and I thought about pressing Luke to at least give me a hint. *But if someone was going to kill him, then they would have done it before he met with me the first time*, I reasoned with myself. Besides, he had assured me that he'd already shared his secret squirrel information with others.

"Okay, I'll see you then," I said and hung up.

Cara was waiting up for me when I got home, with Alvin snoring loudly beside her on the couch and Ivy perched on the kitchen counter waiting impatiently for her bedtime snack.

"What a great welcoming committee," I said, giving Cara a kiss.

"Was it worth the trip?"

"Seeing how Darzi lives was worth the trip. I should have become a pathologist," I said, and proceeded to give her all the details about Darzi's lifestyle.

"What about the case?"

"Everything points to suicide. And, if half of what his parents said is true, then it was a real tragedy, but…" I shook my head sadly. It was impossible to know what drove some people to make a decision that wrecked so many lives.

CHAPTER FIVE

Figuring that, despite his enthusiasm, Luke's evidence would be something less than overwhelming, I didn't give it a lot of thought when I got to the office on Thursday morning. My first order of business was to contact Eddie Thompson, my old CI.

"Larry!" he said excitedly into the phone. I held it away from my ear to protect my hearing, thinking that I sometimes missed the morose, suspicious addict he'd been when I first met him.

"I need to talk to you about some of your homies down in the Ditch."

"Oh, man, I don't go down there no more."

"I know. I just want to talk. Are you going to be around this afternoon?"

"I got a meeting this evening, but nothing much before that."

"See you then," I told him.

I spent the morning closing out some of my own cases, including an assault by an adult on his father and a hit-and-run accident. At eleven-thirty, I got a text from Luke saying that he was about ten minutes away. I told him I'd meet him in the parking lot.

As I came outside, I saw Darlene walking toward me, waving her phone in the air.

"Marcy's on her way," she said.

"It's still in the Southern Gulf. They still can't be sure," I said dismissively.

"It picked up speed overnight. Besides, my grandmother says it's going to come up here and she's never wrong."

"You're pulling my leg."

"I'm telling you. That woman has lived in South Florida all of her life and has an uncanny ability to predict where hurricanes are going to go."

"Hurricanes have a mind of their own."

"Gramma says it's coming to Tallahassee," Darlene said and waggled her finger at me.

"Does she say what category it's going to be when it hits?" I challenged her.

"I'm just sayin' you might want to stock up on batteries and bottle some water," Darlene said, walking past me into the office.

I checked my own phone. If the storm *was* coming, then we still had a couple of days according to the most recent projections from the National Hurricane Center. I thought about all the hurricanes I'd already been through. My first big storm was Kate. I couldn't remember it since I was less than a year old at the time, but Mom had used to love telling me how I'd spent my first Thanksgiving without electricity. In the Big Bend, Kate was still the hurricane to beat for the older generation. She'd struck in late November and no recorded hurricane before or since has hit the United States that late in the season. It had shaken Tallahassee to its core, bringing down hundreds, if not thousands, of trees and taking out just about everyone's power for days.

The worst year I could remember was 2004, when Florida had been pummeled by a series of unpredictable storms. Our area had caught parts of a tropical storm and two of the hurricanes, including Frances, which had moved more slowly than any storm I could remember and had seemed to last for days. We'd been lucky over the last few years, but in Florida it was never a question of if, but when.

"You daydreaming?" Luke asked, coming up behind me.

I turned. "Just taking a trip down hurricane memory lane."

"Marcy. Yeah, I probably need to get back home and batten down the hatches."

"Come on, we'll get some lunch before you head back out and you can tell me where this hunch of yours came from."

Luke followed me to Deep Pit Bar-b-que. As soon as our pork plates and drinks were in front of us, Luke pulled out a copy of a printed email and laid it on the table.

I picked it up and read: *The body of Rudy Lynch was recently found in the woods. Check it out. Could Blake Klein be behind it?* The address of the sender was friend4532@yourmail.net. I frowned.

"I had a techie friend run a check on the email. Apparently, whoever sent it was using some blind ISPs or whatnots to hide their real address," Luke said.

"I'm trying to get my head around this. Assuming that Blake Klein is still alive, then why would he kill Rudy Lynch? Who would know and why would they send this to you? And if it's a hoax, then why? Is there someone out there trying to goad you into writing a story that they can later expose as bunk?"

"Sure, I've got a few enemies. Not that I try and piss people off, but Pelican Island is a small place. People are always getting upset about something I included, or something I didn't include, in the paper. Cost of doing business."

"Was there something about the way you reported the Klein story that could have particularly pissed someone off?"

"There was maybe a little grumbling that I included so much about the spy cameras he'd put into the houses he managed. Some folks thought it might make tourists nervous if they knew about it," Luke answered.

"Anyone specific?"

"Guy Striker, who owns Guy's Rentals. He told me I shouldn't bite the tourism hand that feeds us, but he's just a big bag of wind."

"The only hard evidence that even hints at Rudy's death not being a suicide is the fact there weren't any pills in the vomit recovered from the bag or the throat of the victim. If he voluntarily took the pills, then he would have had to crush them up first."

"There you go!" Luke said. His enthusiasm confirmed what I already knew—Luke wanted this to be something more mysterious than a suicide.

"Whoa there, tiger. There's always outlier evidence. We'll just need to see what the toxicology report has to say."

"Can't you contact FDLE?" Luke was having a hard time containing his excitement. He had obviously been working hard to keep his opinions bottled up until I'd had a chance to look everything over, but now that I'd seen the files, he seemed determined to press his view of the case.

"I don't really think you want me to call and tell them that I've seen the files on their case and want them to press forward with a homicide investigation," I reminded him.

"Oh, yeah." He looked deflated. "I forgot you don't have any better access to this case than I do."

"Or that you're supposed to have. You, me and your informant could get in a whole bunch of trouble for this. If we had a smoking gun, then maybe we could find a way to get FDLE to act on it and not get in too much trouble. But if you start stirring the pot without just cause, you're going to royally piss them off." I decided I needed to be as blunt with him as possible.

"I see your point. Damn it. I don't know. It's just that since we didn't find Klein's body, it's been niggling at me."

"The way his boat wrecked and the thorough search performed by the Coast Guard was enough to convince me that Klein didn't survive."

"He was such a slippery dick," Luke said, frowning.

"I'd have to agree with you there. If he was still alive then I would absolutely want to catch him and have him punished for his crimes. But this," I indicated the email, "just isn't enough to get me to go on a wild goose chase."

"Sorry," he said, his eyes downcast. He picked at his French fries.

"You did the right thing. I'm glad you didn't just ignore the email. Can I keep this?" I asked, picking up the paper.

"Sure."

"I'll talk to our tech guy and see if he has any thoughts on how we could find out who sent it."

"Great!" Luke was the perfect example of a guy who never grew up, or gave up, for that matter.

"In the meantime, I'll give you some homework. Dig through Rudy Lynch's background and see what you can find. If you discover a link to Blake Klein, then we can follow that to wherever it leads. But don't limit yourself to trying to find connections to Klein. Fight your bias."

"Excellent, dude. I'll dive right into this."

Before this talk, I'd intended to dampen Luke's enthusiasm for the idea that Lynch's death was murder, but he was like a fifty-year-old kid. I almost felt bad disappointing him, but I really hoped we'd be able to put the whole thing to bed soon.

I looked at the email again when I got back to my desk. Blake Klein had been one evil son of a bitch. He'd videotaped people and blackmailed them and, when things had started to go sideways on him, he'd started killing. I really did hope that his bones were rotting on the bottom of the Gulf.

As promised, I took the email down to Lionel West, our IT guy. His office was a well air-conditioned room that was way too small for the bones of all the computers, laptops and phones stacked around him. The plans for the building renovation included a new forensic IT room, which would have its own evidence storage area. The current situation was a pain in the ass. Lionel had to check evidence out when he wanted to work on it and check it back in before he left the office.

A sign on the closed door invited me in. I opened it to see Lionel hunched over a laptop, wearing headphones. He waved me to a chair that I had to clear of various screwdrivers and disk drives. I watched him work for a couple minutes as soundwaves moved across the screen and he rapidly clicked a mouse. Never in a million years would I have had the patience for whatever type of tedious work he was doing.

"Do you have something new for me?" he asked, taking off his headphones.

"Not really. Looks like you have enough work to do anyway," I said, nodding toward the laptop. While I didn't have any patience, I did have more than my share of curiosity.

"This is a 911 call. You can just hear the victim in the background and Pete wanted me to enhance it if I could. The perp is claiming that the victim was attacking her."

"Who called 911?"

"She did. After she stabbed the guy five times. He claims that she was pissed 'cause she found some text messages from another girl on his phone and just went bonkers on him. It sure does sound like he's in shock in the background of the call. He says 'What the hell?' and 'Why the ef did you do that?' about three times."

"Charming couple," I said and handed him a copy of the email. "We are officially on break."

"Really?"

"This is someone else's case, but let's just say I have an interest in it. When you read it, you'll know why. A friend of mine got this email. Is there any way to trace it back to the source?"

"I'd need to get into your friend's email."

"That can be arranged."

"Off the record, right?"

"Yep."

"That means off the payroll."

"What do you want?" I said suspiciously.

"I want to go to the academy," Lionel said flatly.

"Why?" I asked, genuinely astonished. "You're going to have more room when the renovations get done."

"But if I want to move up in the department then I need to be a law enforcement officer. I just want to spend a couple of years on the street." He sounded sure of himself and I tried to picture the thin, spiffy dresser writing tickets and busting shoplifters. Not that I particularly looked the part of a hardened deputy myself.

"You want me to write a letter of recommendation?"

"Exactly. And maybe talk to some of the powers that be and see if I can't go on the department's dime. My girlfriend and I are planning to get married next year, so I'm strapped for cash."

"And, trust me, you want to get the academy done before you're married." Going through the law enforcement academy wasn't quite as tough and it didn't take as long as, say, medical school, but there was certainly pressure to perform. "You know I'm not on very good terms with my dad right now?"

I think Lionel blushed, though it was hard to discern with his darker skin.

"The nepotism billboard was a low blow," he said. "Whatever you can do would be great."

"No problem," I said and called Luke. I explained that Lionel would need access to his email and then left the two of them to work out the details.

I looked at my watch and decided it was time to go see Eddie.

He had a garage apartment at Albert Griffin's house. When I pulled up, Mr. Griffin was at the curb getting his mail.

"Larry! How's it going?"

I walked with him up to his porch. I thought that he seemed to be moving a little slower today. *He is getting up in years*, I reminded myself.

"I'm good. How are you doing, Mr. Griffin?"

"Eddie's been a great help around here. Seems to be traveling the straight and narrow."

"Glad to hear it."

"You might be interested to know I'm writing an article on Adams County elections. There have been some real doozies. In 1954, Jack Cameron was running for mayor and Bud Schneider threw a pitcher of water at him during a debate, calling him a Commie."

"Who won?"

"Cameron, by twenty votes. But Schneider never believed he lost that election."

"It's good to know that this isn't the worst election we've had."

"Not by a long shot. In 1878 the sheriff was shot down the day of the election. Took place at a polling station which normally served as a church. None of the ten witnesses saw who pulled the trigger, or at least they wouldn't admit it. The sheriff had gotten himself into some pretty sorry situations, including enforcing eviction notices on folks still trying to recover from the Civil War."

"With luck, there won't be any lead flying on election day."

"Trust the people. Your dad is well liked and most folks know that this McCune character is an ass," Mr. Griffin said. I knew that he kept his ear pretty close to the ground so hearing him say this gave me a bit of reassurance.

"Is Eddie here?"

"Up in his apartment."

I went up the stairs on the side of the garage and rapped on the door vigorously. I had no intention of opening the door until I was invited in. One of the issues that had made Eddie's teenage years with his family so hellish had been their discovery that he was a crossdresser. Knowing about his proclivities, I wasn't going to open the door and risk seeing something I wouldn't be able to unsee.

"Yeah, coming!" Eddie yelled from the other side of the door.

When he let me in, I took one look at him and knew that he really was staying sober. He was carrying around an extra fifteen pounds. When he'd been messing around with drugs, he'd been almost anorexic.

"Putting on some weight," I said good-naturedly.

"Maybe a little."

"Seriously, you look like you're doing well."

"Wow! You must really need something. I told you I don't mix with those boys in the Ditch."

"Don't worry. This is about a robbery that happened down there, but what I need from you is just to find out if there is any word on the street about other dealers who've been robbed."

"They've noticed that I don't use anymore. Besides, most of the folks that were my regular suppliers are in jail. Hell, one of them died last month from an overdose."

"I understand, but I know you still hang around outside the Fast Mart. I just want to know what they're talking about."

"My sponsor told me I wasn't maintaining enough distance from some of my former associates," Eddie said.

"I get it. And you know that I support your sobriety," I said, while pulling out my wallet. "How much support do you think you need? Be reasonable."

"I've been looking for a regular job," he said and hesitated for a moment before adding, "Forty dollars. I need to help out with the groceries."

Honestly, I felt like a heel for asking him. Eddie had almost been killed the month before trying to help me with a case, and I'd promised Mr. Griffin and Cara that I would stop using him as an informant. I told myself that all I was doing in this case was asking him to keep his ears open. "Maybe I can help you get a real job," I said, handing him two twenties.

"I'll see what I can hear." He paused. "No, I guess I'll hear what I can hear."

"Whichever. Just get back with me as soon as you can."

When I got home that evening, Cara was already there and had her face glued to her phone, which wasn't normal.

"Hello?" I said, walking over to her.

"Sorry, just obsessing over Marcy."

"What's the latest?"

"We're still in the center of the projected cone. According to the forecasts, we could get effects as early as Saturday."

"Hurricanes can change course at any time," I said, remembering some of the sudden turns of recent storms. "That's why they use a cone for their predictions."

"What worries me is the fact they're predicting it to be a Category 4 by the time it gets close to our coast."

"We're eighty miles inland and almost two hundred feet above sea level, so it will lose a lot of its punch by the time it reaches us," I said, but couldn't help adding, "Though a Category 2 would be bad enough."

The text alert on my phone went off.

"What?" Cara asked, seeing the look on my face as I read the message.

"I have to be at an emergency management meeting at nine in the morning."

"Why are you on the emergency management team?"

"Pete should be since he's the senior investigator, but he's already on the tac team as their sniper, plus he's the firearms instructor, so he suggested me for the role."

"Why do they need an investigator?"

"My job is to make sure that the evidence and case files are secure and there's no interruption to the chain of custody. The only thing that's been cool about it is that I got to look over the plans for the addition they're getting ready to build, including the stuff Lionel requested for IT evidence. He suggested some improvements that would help keep all the electronic evidence dry and cool during a power outage."

"So you'll have to go in if the storm comes?"

"I'd be on duty anyway, but with this assignment I'll basically have to sleep at the office. I'll have Charley Wright, who works in maintenance, with me to help in an emergency. Of course, the rest of the team will be across the street at the emergency management operations center."

"Where is that?"

"You've seen it. It's that addition to the right side of the jail. It was built just after Andrew and upgraded about five years ago. It's got a huge generator and an area for dispatch to work."

"But you don't send deputies out during a hurricane."

"True, not during the worst of it. But we keep dispatch open so people can call and be talked through an emergency, if necessary, and also to be ready to send out first responders as soon as the winds die down."

"Your dad will be at the meeting," she reminded me, reaching out and touching my arm.

I was about to answer when I got another text. I showed it to Cara. It was from Dad and read: *Be in my office at eight tomorrow.*

"I guess he doesn't want us to meet for the first time in a while in public. Probably wants to vent a little beforehand," I said, feeling grim at the prospect.

"Your dad's under a lot of pressure," Cara said, determined to play peacemaker.

"The trouble is that I really do feel guilty about the whole McCune thing."

"You've both just got to let it go."

"Easier said than done. I keep asking myself why I had to be such a hardass with McCune."

"He got under your skin when you were hunting a killer."

"Okay, Miss I-have-all-the-answers. How do I make it right?"

"Some things you just have to ride out."

"If Marcy comes to visit, I'll have two storms to ride out."

CHAPTER SIX

The next morning, I stopped outside the glass door stenciled with the Adams County seal and "Sheriff Ted Macklin" and took a deep breath, vowing to take the browbeating with quiet dignity and grace, just like in *Young Frankenstein*.

Dad's assistant didn't say a word as she waved me into the office. When I opened the door, I was met by the black-and-white menace that my dad called a dog. Mauser, his one-hundred-and-ninety pound Great Dane, hadn't seen me in a while and this exponentially increased his enthusiasm to compensate for the lost time. I was knocked back against the door, but managed to give my furry brother his due. His joy was too much to fight.

"Okay, you big lunk, that's enough," I told him, which translated into "more, more," in Mauser-speak. He bumped his shoulder into my waist three more times and shook his head, flinging slobber all over me, before he was satisfied that I had been properly reprimanded for not coming to see him more often.

Dad had stayed quiet through all of this and, when I looked over at him, he was just standing behind his desk with a frown on his face. The frown wasn't a bad sign—he almost always frowned—but the fact that he was standing wasn't good. Normally, when he called me into his office, he'd sit behind his large desk and handle several other tasks while giving me the least amount of attention he could. This often annoyed me, but now I remembered how much worse it was to receive the full focus of his attention.

"Those billboards," he started, but then he seemed to run out of words... or at least words he could say out loud.

"I know—" I blurted, but he held up a hand.

"Stop. It's too late to do anything about it. Now I have to deal with damage control. The *Tallahassee Democrat* is doing a story on the billboards. At least they called and warned me about it. I told them I'd talk to them after the emergency management meeting this morning. At some point, they're going to want to talk to you." I watched his hands clench and unclench as he talked. "I called you in here to remind you to soft-pedal any emotions you might have toward McCune. He's a full-fledged ass, but we can't call him out in public. Just don't talk bad about him. That's what the reporters want. Conflict makes a story. We have to act like it's not a big deal, as ridiculous as that is."

Everything I could think of to say was stupid. *Are you scared of losing the election? Are you pissed at me? What can I do to help?* I already knew the answers: *Yes. Hell yes!* and *Nothing.*

"At least you're getting the construction started on the addition to the office," I said lamely.

"That's something, I guess. The county is only having to pony up twenty-five percent of the funds. A federal law enforcement grant is picking up the rest of the tab. I just hope I'm still here when the job is done."

"I'll be the model of decorum if any reporters contact me," I said and meant it.

"Thanks," Dad said, and it didn't even sound too sarcastic.

Honestly, Dad could have retired right then and done very well if he'd wanted to. He had a pension and plenty of savings, and he could have picked up quite a bit of consulting work if he wanted to stay busy. But for him I knew it was all about the other people who'd be displaced if he lost the election. I really didn't want to lose my job either. Over the last year, I'd grown into being at least a fair investigator. I'd stumbled into my career in law enforcement as a way to help Dad out of his grief over losing my mother, but now I finally felt like it was the right career for me. And I didn't want to work for Charles Maxwell. He was competent enough, but he was a jerk and he didn't deserve to be sheriff.

"Of course Maxwell's going to be at the meeting this morning." I hadn't meant to say it out loud, but it was something to consider. As chief of the Calhoun Police Department, no matter how small it was, he automatically had a seat on the emergency management team.

"Not a problem. I have to give the man credit. He's already called and apologized for the billboards. It's not like they're his fault."

"He didn't say he was dropping out of the race, did he?"

"No," Dad said, and I could almost see the hint of a smile. "That ain't going to happen. Get out of here. I'll see you at the meeting."

Half an hour later I was seated in the emergency management operations center next to the jail. The name made it sound more impressive than it was. In reality it was a large, cafeteria-sized room with several tables and lots of electrical and USB outlets, as well as half a dozen LED monitors hung around the walls. One section was set aside with tables, chairs and computers where dispatch would be headquartered.

I nodded and said hello to several of my fellow county employees sitting around me. There were folks I knew from the fire department, EMS, road maintenance and several representatives of the power cooperative that serviced most of the county.

Dad arrived with Mauser in tow, which surprised me a

little. He often brought the big goof to the office, but he didn't normally take him to meetings. Dad went to the front of the room as fast as he could while greeting people and letting everyone pet and make over Mauser, who was basking in all of the attention.

Chief Maxwell was the last of the officials to come into the center. Finally, there were half a dozen people standing at the front of the room, including the city and county managers. I expected the meeting to start at any time when I heard Cara ask if the seat next to me was taken.

"What are you doing here?" I asked.

But before she could answer, there was a commotion at the front of the room. I looked up and saw Mauser plowing his way through the chairs toward us, dragging Dad behind him. Eventually, Dad gave up and let Mauser loose to the amusement of everyone.

The dog came bounding up to Cara, doing a little hop-step in front of her as if he needed to get her attention. Cara was on his short list of favorite people. Already amped up from the crowd, he couldn't control himself when he saw her.

With everyone watching, Cara sheepishly greeted Mauser and took his leash.

"He can stay back there," Dad said when she started to stand up. "I guess we can get this meeting started. I brought my moose along for a reason. After the meeting, we're going to be recording several PSAs related to our emergency management plan. Mauser is going to assist me and Bud Emery from the humane society in announcing that two of the county's emergency shelters will be able to accommodate pets. The PSA will talk about what evacuees should bring for their pets. Speaking of pets, one of the guests here is Mauser's friend, Cara, from Dr. Barnhill's clinic. The clinic will be providing staff volunteers to help with animal intake at the shelters and Cara will be working here during the storm to coordinate efforts between the shelters, the clinic and animal rescue groups."

"You didn't tell me any of this," I said in a whisper to Cara.

"I didn't know until I got to work this morning. Apparently Dr. Barnhill was contacted by Bud from the humane society," she said, petting Mauser, who was looking up at her adoringly.

Dad continued with introductions. I was familiar with most of the people, but the doctor from the local clinic was new. The clinic was run by the hospital in Tallahassee and doctors frequently rotated in and out.

"Dr. Greg Patrick will be advising us on any health issues associated with a crisis. In the case of a hurricane, that will most likely involve possible contamination of drinking water and any diseases from flood waters or dead animals," Dad said. Dr. Patrick was a tall, lean man with a neatly trimmed full beard. He smiled and nodded when introduced, looking at ease in the spotlight.

After a review of staff assignments and schedules, the county manager provided an update on Marcy's latest status.

"I talked with the governor's emergency management coordinator and what he's hearing from the National Hurricane Center is that the storm is expected to make landfall about one hundred miles to the west of us, either late Saturday or early Sunday. It's weakened a bit, but the current prediction is for a Category 3 at landfall. This is a big storm and we could get some of the first bands as early as this evening." He paused and scanned the room. "And remember, even if we aren't directly impacted by the storm, coastal communities have already started evacuations and our shelters will be open to those folks as well."

Dad addressed the room again. "Okay, this meeting is adjourned. I'm going to open the doors to the journalists for about fifteen minutes and then everyone involved with the PSAs should meet in the small office at the back of the building."

As the room cleared out, I saw Maxwell walk over to Dad and they talked for a minute. Oddly, this craziness with

McCune seemed to have brought them together. Of course, neither of them would have allowed any animosity to interfere with their duties. On the other hand, both of them had a strong stubborn streak. If they were seen being cordial, then it meant they were putting in a bit more effort than just setting aside their differences for the sake of their jobs.

"Dr. Barnhill gave me these notes from Dr. Betty Horvath," Cara told me. "I'm supposed to make sure the information gets out." As she held up a piece of paper, Mauser tried to eat it.

"You aren't starving," I said, using my hand to block the oaf while I looked at the list. It was a series of suggestions for people who owned livestock. Horvath was the area's large-animal vet. "Dr. Horvath ought to be your vet, you big horse," I told Mauser.

Dad came over to us, but before Cara could give him the list, Mauser launched into him with an enthusiastic greeting like he hadn't seen Dad in a month.

"Good boy," Dad said to him and shocked me by winking at me. It didn't take me long to figure out what he was up to. A few newsmen and women were coming in through the back door, followed by camera operators. Dad took Mauser's leash from Cara and headed their way. Much excitement ensued as Mauser made a spectacle of himself. One of the newsmen was obviously not a fan of dogs and went to find someone else to talk to.

"I didn't get a chance to give him the notes from Dr. Horvath," Cara said.

"You may as well wait. Dad has to deal with the reporters."

"I could have held on to Mauser for him," she said, and then light dawned in her eyes. "He's using Mauser as a distraction!"

"Exactly," I said, watching the reporters trying to talk to Dad while Mauser bumped into them and stepped all over their feet. I saw one of them look up and eye me. Eager to make my escape, I said, "Let's go on back to where they're recording the PSAs and you can give it to him there."

As we worked our way toward the back of the building we ran into Floyd Krueger, the head of the county's planning department, who was heading toward Dad and the reporters.

"Hi, Larry, I thought I'd go rescue your dad," he told me with a grin.

We'd been on good terms since my last year on patrol when I had helped him out with his teenage son. I'd stopped a car full of kids on a Friday night. The driver was intoxicated and the rest of the boys were in various states of sobriety. I'd called all their families and had made a special effort to ensure Floyd's son got delivered to him. Not because Floyd worked for the county, but because his son was the youngest in a group of kids that was looking for trouble.

"How's Chris?" I asked, remembering his son's name.

"He just might make it to college next year. One more year," he said, holding up his hand with his fingers crossed.

"Floyd, this is Cara Laursen."

"I know Mr. Krueger," Cara said. "He has the world's sweetest Golden Retriever, which is saying something."

"And you and Dr. Barnhill do a great job spoiling him," Floyd said before he walked away.

We went into the small room where a young man and woman were setting up recording equipment for the PSAs. A large Adams County Emergency Management logo had been mounted on the back wall and two large lights with umbrellas were facing it to shine on whoever was on camera.

"Are you two doing a PSA?" the woman asked. She was petite with short hair and a crooked grin.

"Noooo," I said, backing away. "But she might be," I said, shoving Cara under the video bus.

"I'm not so sure…" Cara started.

"Step over here so we can check out the lighting," the woman said, while the man pulled a professional camera out of a hard case.

Cara nervously stood on the marks she'd indicated and

waited as the team worked, exchanging only a few cryptic words while they adjusted the lights and focused the camera.

"That's great," the woman said, just as the door opened and a dozen people came in. Leading the pack was Mauser.

"What the hell is that?" the guy asked. He was tall, in his early thirties and sporting a man-bun, and he looked like he wanted to make a run for the door.

Mauser instantly homed in on him as the one person in the room who wasn't interested in meeting him. The Dane was always challenged by anyone who didn't make happy sounds when they saw him. It took some calming words from Dad and demonstrations of Mauser's placid nature to get the cameraman to pet him and satisfy Mauser's ego.

"Bud Emery is running late. Cara, would you mind helping me with the PSA about the shelters that will take pets?" Dad asked.

Cara looked nervous, but after a moment she swallowed and nodded. "I've got this too," she said, handing Dad the list from Dr. Horvath. He scanned through it.

"Yeah, it's probably a good idea to paint a phone number and your name on the side of your horses and cows. I remember having to run down some loose animals after Kate. Okay, let's do two PSAs for pets, one for the shelters and one with advice for owners of livestock."

"You better not let Finn hear you call him livestock," I said. Dad had two American Quarter Horses, rare twins named Finn and Mac. While he loved them both, Finn and Dad just seemed to click.

"He's not going to like it if I have to spray paint my name on him either," Dad said with a smile. He checked a list on a small table in the corner. "We've got five PSAs to do. Dr. Patrick is up first, then we'll do the pet ones."

We watched Dad and Dr. Patrick take instructions from the cameraman until they were in position and looking in the right direction.

Dr. Patrick didn't look much older than me. It was about time to go in for my yearly physical and it was going to feel odd not having an older doctor, though he seemed like a nice enough guy. He was quite self-confident in front of the camera, telling everyone to make sure they had enough prescription medicines for two weeks and to remember to bring their medicines to the shelter with them. Next he gave out a special number for people who needed medical help if they had to evacuate their homes. Finally, he reminded anyone who used a medical device that ran on electricity to notify the power company of their needs. Dad nodded and gave out the addresses of all the shelters in the county.

"Dr. Patrick did a great job. Why do I have to follow him on stage?" Cara joked.

Despite her fears, she did a fine job as part of a comedy trio with Dad and Mauser.

"You knocked it out of the park," I told her when it was over. "And Mauser was a great model to demonstrate where to paint your information on your livestock."

"That was really embarrassing," Cara said, her face still a bit flushed.

"You're going to have to get over the humble routine when you're a star," I said.

"Stop it," she said, the tone of her voice making it clear I shouldn't push the joke any further.

"Just kidding," I told her and bumped against her playfully. I seldom got to see her insecure side. "When do you start your new position?" I asked.

"I think this was my first assignment."

CHAPTER SEVEN

Cara headed back to the clinic and I walked across the street to the sheriff's office. The construction crew was using a backhoe to bust ground for the new addition. I was impressed with the skill the guy demonstrated as he swung the big bucket around, smashing the asphalt and then digging it out and piling it to one side.

Inside, I found Darlene staring intently at some reports.

"What've you got?" I asked. I wasn't really interested; I was just stalling. I had a couple of my own reports that needed to be written, but I wasn't in the mood to spend the rest of the morning behind the desk.

"I'm going over the reports from Hitdawg's robbery," she said, unusually solemn.

"Something wrong?"

"No. I just can't get it out of my head that this dude is dangerous."

"I agree. But why in particular?"

"Okay, we can agree that young master Hitdawg isn't very book smart. But let's give the devil his due. He's been selling drugs and living on the mean streets of Adams County for a while. But when this goes down he panics and calls 5-0."

"It's probably not the first time he's had a gun pointed in his face either," I said.

"He's been in jail four times on minor offenses since he was an adult. I would imagine that there are a number of run-ins with the law on his sealed juvenile record. He's also named as the victim in one shooting where he had a toe shot off, and a beating that put him in the hospital for a week. Neither time was he the one who reported the attacks. And both times he lied and said he had no idea who the perps were."

"I see your point. You think our guy isn't local?"

"That's what I'm thinking. If he was a local guy gone rogue, then I don't think Rufus would have panicked and called us. He'd have tried to take care of it himself."

"True enough." I picked up my phone. "Let's see if my fly on the wall has any info for us."

I dialed Eddie.

"It's been less than twenty-four hours," was how he answered the phone, but I could tell from his cheery tone that he must have something for me.

"What have you learned?"

"I have to admit, I'm pretty good."

"Quit trying to get a raise," I said, putting the phone on speaker so Darlene could listen in.

"I shouldn't be bragging 'cause I didn't have to do much. The first person I said hi to was dying to talk about this bastard. From what everyone is saying, he's hit a couple of dealers and rolled a dozen buyers. He car-jacked an Escalade from Marco. Not a smart thing to do. Marco is screaming bloody murder."

"No word on who it is?"

"There are a few theories. It's either a cartel guy come to shake things up, a punk from Miami who got run out of town there and has gone loco, or, last but not least, a nig... black guy from Atlanta who thinks he can come here and punk everyone. I've heard all of those and a few more."

"No clear consensus on whether he's black, white or

Hispanic?" I asked, more than a little surprised.

"No. Everyone is pretty sure it's a he. Most have said he's a big guy. Not scared. People say he's calm, not like some buzzed-out addict."

"What kind of clothes does he wear?" Darlene asked.

"Is that Deputy Darlene? Hey, girl! Black, black and more black. Black mask, gloves, gun. Big gun."

"Voice?" I asked.

"Nothing. I think he scares everyone so bad they don't really remember much. The one thing everyone says is that this guy will kill you."

"Has he actually shot anyone?"

"He's shot two people in the leg according to what's on the street, but no one named names, so I wouldn't take that for gospel."

"Thanks, Eddie," I said, then paused. "Make sure Mr. Griffin has what he needs if this hurricane shows up."

"I got that covered. We went to the store last night. Water, batteries, crackers, peanut butter, don't worry."

After I hung up with Eddie, Darlene said, "Let's go make some rounds before we have a dead body. If nothing else, we need to chase this hombre out of the county."

"Alright, pardner. You want to saddle up your horse or mine?" I said in a bad Western drawl.

"Remember the first rule. Don't be an ass."

We took her car. I called dispatch and got the current address for Marco Cabello. He was one of a dirty dozen that we kept an eye on. He knew it and mainly used runners and mules to control his business.

"How's your little side investigation going?" Darlene asked. I'd given her a brief overview after meeting with Luke on Tuesday.

"Luke has an active imagination and I think someone is playing him."

"Was it a suicide?"

"I'll withhold final judgment until the toxicology results comes in, but if it's not, I don't know how you'd ever prove anything different."

"Are we going to try the good-cop/good-cop routine with Mr. Cabello?"

"I don't see why not. This is his problem as much as it is ours."

"No reason to bust his balls for being a victim," Darlene agreed.

"The only reason he might want to hold back is so he can make a play for the guy. But if he can't find him then he can't make an example of him."

We pulled up in front of a well-kept, two-story house in a small development that had been built just before the housing market crashed in 2008. Marco was a funny sort. He could do the tough-guy act, but underneath he always seemed like he just wanted to be a regular guy. I think he saw himself as some sort of Tony Soprano. An unfortunate side effect of us having taken down the Thompson family drug ring was that it had created a vacuum that small-time guys like Marco were rising up to fill.

As we walked to the house, we could hear laughter and the sounds of a party coming from the backyard. Two men answered the door. Both were in their late twenties and both of them were wearing coats, even though the September weather was still warm and humid.

"Yeah?" asked one of the men with a coffin tattoo on his neck.

I showed him my badge while Darlene looked toward the street, watching our backs. "We just want a word with Marco," I said.

"He's having a party," Coffin said.

To prove the point, a boy, maybe nine years old and dripping wet, came running down the hall toward us, waving a pool noodle.

"You aren't Elliott!" he yelled at us and turned to run the other way, laughing. The other man at the door cautioned him not to run in the house.

"We aren't here to disturb him. In fact, we heard he had

some trouble with his Escalade and thought we might help."

"He doesn't need no help," Coffin said.

"Marco might want to talk to them," said the other man, who looked a little older. His ink included a dead man's hand of cards on the side of his neck and spider webs under his chin.

"Go check," Coffin said gruffly.

A couple of uncomfortable minutes later, Marco Cabello came strolling down the hallway, wearing a Hawaiian shirt and khaki shorts. He sported no visible tattoos.

"I know you," he said to me. "Oh, yeah, and you too," he added when he saw that Darlene was with me.

"We heard you had some trouble the other night," I said.

His face flushed and his eyes turned dark. "I don't know what you heard."

"Someone car-jacked your Escalade," I said flatly.

He muttered something in a language I didn't understand.

"Sizzle! Those are some hot words." Darlene apparently *had* understood him.

"I kill this man," Marco said through clenched teeth, all semblance of civility washed away.

"We don't like this guy going around strong-arming people any more than you do," I said.

"Go back to the pool," Marco told Coffin, who turned and left without a word. "We can talk outside," he said to us.

Once we were all standing on his lawn, he looked around to make sure we were alone. "I would pay good money to get a shot at this guy," he said in all seriousness.

"We don't really work that way," I told him. "What do you know about him?"

"He's a nobody. Not from here."

"You mean not from this county or this area?" Darlene asked.

"I got my eyes and ears, man. He's not from anywhere. He's so stupid." Marco drew this last word out into a couple extra syllables. "What'd he take my Escalade for? That's crazy."

"Was he black, white, Hispanic?" I asked.

"Don't know. He was all in black, like some ninja or somethin'."

"Did he shoot one of your men?" Darlene asked, and he gave her a crooked smile.

"No, I'm not going to tell you that. I say he shot somebody, then you be crawling all over us. Hey, is he one of your guys? Is that the play?"

I could tell by his tone and the look in his eye that he didn't seriously believe his own question. The bad guys believed in the rules as much as we did. The minute they thought that a cop would dress in black and shoot one of them in cold blood was the minute when chaos would reign.

"You're flattering yourself," Darlene huffed.

"We need the tag and VIN number of the Escalade. I'm assuming that it was legal," I said.

"Hell yes, it was legal! That was my wife's ride." As soon as he said it, I saw the darkness rise up again in eyes. "If any of my family had been in the car…" He didn't finish the sentence, but it was an emotion we could all understand. "I got the tag. I don't know the VIN number, but I bought it at a dealership in Tallahassee."

"The tag number and a full description will get us what we need."

He left us on the lawn and returned a few minutes later with everything written out neatly on a sheet of paper that had a cute bunny in the corner and said: *Don't forget…* We took the paper and left Marco to return to his family.

"Do you want to risk the Palmetto for lunch?" Darlene asked.

"Why not?"

I texted Pete and told him where we were eating, but he was out at the range doing qualifications with some of the patrol officers. I used the rest of the drive to get dispatch to put out a stolen car BOLO on Marco's Escalade.

Lunch was only a little awkward, with folks either avoiding eye contact with me or coming over to our table and telling me how they were going to vote for Dad, no matter what. At least the wrap and sweet potato fries were good.

"So who is this guy and why is he here?" Darlene pondered after she'd finished off her chicken cheddar sandwich and was making her way through a piece of caramel mud pie.

"Some scout from another gang? They heard about the Thompsons going down, so they decided to send someone over here to see how tough the competition would be if they decided to move in."

"That's not a bad theory. Also, by coming in and stirring the pot, he might cause some infighting that could help weaken the competition more. Not bad at all. You could have had a career running a drug cartel."

"Too much paranoia involved," I said, then I thought about Luke and the email suggesting Blake Klein was alive and still doing bad things. His spy cameras and blackmail operation used paranoia as currency. What if I was wrong and he *had* killed Rudy Lynch? Should I tell Dad? If things were normal then I probably would have mentioned it, but the last thing he needed now was one more thing to worry about. No. The evidence was way too thin to start running around yelling that the sky was falling.

"At least we have a description out on the vehicle he might be driving," Darlene said, and for a minute I thought she was talking about Klein. I shook my head and brought my mind back to the matter at hand.

"I wonder. I would bet money—" Before I could finish, dispatch called to tell us that the burned-out hulk of the Escalade had been found beside the railroad tracks about a mile outside of town. "That was fast," I said, hanging up.

"Color me not surprised," Darlene said. "So much for our one lead."

When we arrived, the SUV was still smoldering. One of our deputies had spotted it shortly after I'd called it in.

"At least we got a break and no one noticed the fire. If

the fire department had gotten here before Martel did, they would have washed everything away with their hoses."

"And he was crappy at arson," I said, looking at the damage that was mostly confined to the front seat.

I called Shantel Williams, the head of our crime scene team.

"Now you want me," she said in greeting, taking me by surprise.

"What? How did I offend thee?" I joked back.

"You asked for Charley to be your emergency management partner while you watch over *my* evidence room."

"I was just being practical. I didn't know how good you would be at getting an HVAC system or a generator up and running again."

"Humph. Maybe you got a small point there. Fine, I'll come out and dust your old car," she said, and hung up after I'd given her the location.

The sky was clouding up and, according to my phone's radar app, dark bands of rain were bearing down on us by the time Shantel showed up with the crime scene van.

"Looks like you and Charley are going to be camping out together sooner rather than later," she said, looking at the sky as she got out of the van.

"Latest reports say that Marcy is definitely headed for landfall a little to our west," Darlene said, looking at her phone. Storm tracking was a Florida pastime during hurricane season, but it could become downright obsessive when a storm was near.

"We flagged some tire tracks and a footprint," I told Shantel as she started to assemble her equipment.

We helped her as much as we could, hoping to beat the rain. She was able to get a palm print from the roof of the car on the passenger side, and a few fingerprints from the rear seats. Of course, those probably had nothing to do with our suspect, but it was better to be thorough.

"Let's tape up the driver's window and have it towed to

the impound lot," Shantel said. "If you want me to do a full sweep of the car, I can do it there."

"So far it's only an armed robbery and car-jacking. We'll wait on collecting hair and fiber until after the storm," I said.

We were following the tow truck bearing the Escalade out onto the road when the sky opened up and rain poured down in buckets.

Darlene and I had just walked into the office when we heard text message alerts going off throughout the building. We were being told that all deputies would go on twelve-hour shifts starting at seven in the morning in preparation for dealing with Marcy.

It was late afternoon, but I decided I wanted to touch base with Charley before I left for the day. As frequently happens with storm bands, the rain had already stopped and I found him outside working on a drainage issue.

Charley Wright didn't look much like a maintenance man. He was a fit forty-year-old who rode his bike to work every morning and had helped Lionel install upgrades to the department's security system. He'd come to work at the department two years earlier after a nasty divorce from his wife.

"I guess we're going to be bunk mates," Charley said as he rammed a plumber's snake up the drainpipe. "I get this clear, it will help. We've been having water flowing back onto the roof with this stopped up."

"Plan on staying tomorrow and the next night," I told him.

"Fine by me. I don't have any family to worry about." He pulled on the snake and out came a smelly, tangled mess of leaves and plants that had been rooting inside the pipe. "I'll make sure we have batteries and tools. I ordered a dozen tarps at the beginning of hurricane season and had the generator and underground tank filled the day before yesterday. We should be as prepared as we can be. Ronny and Alberto can start boarding up the windows in the morning."

I thanked him and headed home, hoping to get some sleep before we went on war footing. When I reached our trailer in the woods, I saw that Cara's car wasn't there. Checking my phone, I saw a text she'd sent while I was driving: *I'll be late. Trying to get things ready here at the clinic. Love.*

I fed Alvin and Ivy and wondered what we were going to do with them during the storm while we were both working. The small doublewide wasn't the most storm-worthy house, but it had been put on the property after Andrew, so the tie-downs were up to code and I'd replaced the roof when I bought the place. The trees that surrounded it were my biggest concern. They were large live oaks, some that had seen a hundred and fifty years of storms and were still standing, but they were getting old.

I'd talk with Cara about it when she got home. Maybe boarding them at the vet would be the best solution. From the narrow-eyed laser stare of doom I got from Ivy, I had the feeling she already knew what I was thinking.

I had a bowl of soup and a sandwich ready for Cara when she walked in. She dug into it gratefully.

"We're going to have so many animals from our clients," she said when I brought up the idea of boarding them at the vet. "I think they'll be fine here. Wind is the only real issue."

"Alvin is going to need to go for a walk," I reminded her.

"Your dad has a generator, right? What's he doing with Mauser?"

"One way to find out," I said and called him. It turned out that he'd already made plans for Jamie, his frequent dog-sitter, to stay at the house with Mauser.

"I don't see why you can't bring Alvin and Ivy over too," Dad said. Before I could thank him, I got another call and looked at the number. It was Darlene. I told Dad I had to go and switched over.

"Oh, honey, do we have a mess," she said. "I'm at the Ditch looking at a body that could be our armed robber."

"On my way."

CHAPTER EIGHT

Rain came down sporadically as we stood on the porch of Hitdawg's house.

"We covered the body the best we could," Darlene fretted. "But with it being on the slope of the ditch, the water is just washing under the tarp. If we'd tried to stop it, we would have made an even bigger mess."

"We" referred to her and Deputy Julio Ortiz, who'd been the first to respond to the call of a passed-out drunk.

"You can only do what you can do," I said philosophically, though I agreed that this was going to be a royal mess. I didn't see any way to set up lights in the rain without running the risk of electrocuting ourselves.

"There's no way to put up a tent with all that vegetation and the incline," Julio said, echoing my train of thought. He was holding the beam of his Maglite on the tarp-covered body.

"What makes you think that's our robber?" I asked. Since there was no way to go over to the body without making things worse, I'd decided to wait for Dr. Darzi's people to come and do their corpse dance.

"He was dressed completely in black, I didn't recognize him and he had a hole in the back of his head. Oh, yeah, and don't forget that his body was found at the scene of one of the robberies. Though I could be wrong," Darlene said snarkily.

"Point made. Hitdawg is no genius, but if he killed the guy, then why would he leave the body here?"

"Hitdawg didn't do this. Even he's not stupid enough to commit murder in front of his own house on the same day he posts bail for another crime. Besides, look at the way the underbrush has been disturbed all the way down the hill. I think the guy was dumped here."

I could see flashing lights up by the road. "The roadkill boys are here," I said. I pulled my yellow raincoat hood over my head and carefully made my way across the muddy cinderblock path up from the ditch.

Darzi's assistants, Linda and Ann, were waiting by the van when I got to the road. Both wore hooded raincoats and looked up at me as the rain came down harder.

"Is there a tent over the body?" Linda was almost shouting to be heard over the rain.

"No. It's down there. No way to cover it up except by throwing a tarp over it," I told them and got frustrated looks in return.

"That's going to make everything a lot harder. Cut this rain off and we'll get to work," Linda said, shaking her head.

"I think Darzi is rubbing off on you," I told her.

"Nah, it's the job. Stick enough thermometers up the ass of enough corpses and you're either going to get a sense of humor or become a very dark person. She's going dark," Ann said, receiving a light punch on the shoulder from Linda in return.

"Are they still not paying you?" I asked Ann, who had been working as an intern in Darzi's office for several months.

"There are rumors of a vacancy," she said, holding up crossed fingers.

"Get the big umbrella. We need to get to work," Linda told her.

When we got to the body, Ann opened an umbrella that was at least five feet across and held it over the corpse while Linda bent to examine the victim.

"We're going to lose evidence. No way around it," Linda said. She bagged up his hands and feet as best she could. When she started to pull his pants down, I decided to return to the porch. Darlene was on the radio when I got there.

"I've put out a BOLO on our buddy Hitdawg and his car," she said. "Julio and I were going to canvass the Ditch and see if anyone will admit to seeing anything."

"That's unlikely," I said, watching the women work over the body. The rain was letting up and they had finished with his temperature. "I'm going to see if our victim has any ID on him."

I walked back to the body, putting on latex gloves and pulling out a few evidence bags that I'd put in my pocket.

"I want to check for ID."

"Be our guest," Linda said affably.

I found a wallet, two Powerball tickets and a few coins. No car keys. I asked Linda to shine her light on the wallet while I looked through it. The driver's license was in the name of Clark Banner. I took it out of the plastic case. The picture matched the body, but unfortunately the license was a fake. I put it back and looked at the credit cards. They were also for Clark Banner, but I couldn't tell if they were real or not. When I opened the money compartment, I saw two hundred dollars and a business card. Looking at the card, I felt my stomach turn over. It read: *Blake Klein, Real Estate Management*. Cursing under my breath, I put the wallet in one evidence bag and the card in another and walked back to Darlene and Julio. *What the hell?* I thought.

"What you got, top gun?" Darlene asked.

"Fake ID for someone named Clark Banner," I said, trying to decide if I wanted to tell her about the business card.

"Clark Kent, Bruce Banner," Julio said with a shake of his head. "I think you got a comic book fan."

"Great," I said with a full dose of sarcasm. "Would you go start with the interviews?"

"No problem," he responded and headed in the direction of the closest neighbors. Their lights were on, but none of them had stuck their heads out, even though there were flashing lights next door.

"There's more," I said, and went on to tell Darlene everything about Luke Garner's suspicions and the business card I'd just found.

"Ain't the world a funny place?" she said. "You were there when Klein's boat got torn up. I thought you said he was dead."

"I'd have sworn he couldn't have survived all that. The violence of the wreck and then hitting the water. And it's not just that. If he was unconscious for even a minute or two, he would have drowned."

"Both of us have rolled up on accidents and seen cars that were bent and mangled so badly you wouldn't imagine that anyone could come out of them alive. I remember two years ago, I was working an accident. The traffic was stopped in both directions when an old Ford Bronco came around a curve, going way too fast to stop before rear-ending the cars that were waiting on the first accident. I heard the brakes, looked up and saw the driver swerve onto the shoulder to avoid the cars. He lost control and that old tank flipped three times before landing upside down. I called for another ambulance and went running, thinking there was going to be blood and guts everywhere. But nope. By the time I'd run forty yards, the kid was climbing out of the Bronco like he was getting off a carnival ride. Only had a couple bruises."

"I know what you mean. But Klein being thrown into the water… And there was a huge search that started almost immediately and found nothing…" I shook my head.

"It *is* odd that you get wind of him twice in less than a week," she said.

Her words gave me a bad feeling in the pit of my

stomach. Pulling out my phone, I dialed Cara.

"Hey, you on your way home?" she asked, sounding drowsy.

"Sorry to wake you."

"I was just reading and dozed off. I haven't gone to bed yet."

"Look, I don't want to scare you, but I want you to double-check all the doors and windows. Make sure the place is locked up. I'll stay on the line while you do it."

"What's this all about?" I could hear her getting up and moving around while we talked.

"I'll tell you all about it when I get home. Have you walked Alvin already?"

"Yes, he's done his business for the night."

"Make sure you have your gun nearby."

"Now you're scaring me."

"A bad guy might be in the area. I'll just feel better knowing you're locked up safe," I told her. I wasn't looking forward to explaining everything about Klein and his blackmail operation on Pelican Island.

"Okay. How much longer do you think you'll be?"

"A while," I said, though I wanted nothing more than to go straight home, even if it meant having a very awkward conversation with Cara. I was worried that Klein might have decided to target us, which reminded me of the other person I needed to talk to.

"Call me when you're on the way home. I'll be up."

"Try and get some sleep. With the storm coming, the next couple days could be rough."

"I'll try. Love you."

After Cara hung up, I looked at my phone for a moment, took a deep breath and called Dad.

"What?" he answered.

"We might have a situation," I said, and went into a quick and dirty explanation of the information Luke had brought to me and what I'd just found on the body of the dead armed robber.

"Blake Klein. I wouldn't have thought that was possible," he said. I could picture the anger in Dad's green eyes as he thought of Klein loose in his county. "It is what it is. Put out a BOLO on him. Run a records check to see if his social security number or anything else has been used since his presumed death. If so, you'd think it would have triggered a notification to the FBI as they still have an active warrant for him, but this kind of thing gets missed all the time."

"You might want to let Genie know. She was down there with us too."

"She's here," he said, which fell squarely in the TMI box. I'd had a little trouble adjusting to the idea of him having a girlfriend, having never seen him in a serious relationship in the more than ten years since my mom had died. But now, with everything he'd had to deal with in the last few months, I was glad that he had a companion. Also, I'd noticed he didn't ride me quite as much. Another benefit.

"That's probably best."

"She and her son are going to stay here during the storm. They'll be able to help Jamie watch the animals while I'm at work. Besides, if they stayed in Tallahassee, there's a good chance they'd lose power, which shouldn't be a problem here since I put in the automatic propane generator. As far as this Klein situation goes, I want you to follow it to the ground. Of course, you're going to have to wait for the hurricane to go through before you can get your teeth into it."

"Don't worry. Now I really need to know if he's still alive."

"Do what you can tonight. I'll see you in the morning," he said.

Darlene had wandered over to where Linda and Ann were working on the body. I joined them. "Anything you can tell us?" I asked.

"There's a gunshot wound to the head, but you know the routine," Linda said.

"Nothing official until the autopsy."

"You got it. But just between us girls, I'd say the gunshot is your cause of death. The amount of blood suggests that the victim was alive when the wound was inflicted, and the damage caused by the bullet suggests that he didn't live for more than a minute after he was shot."

"Any idea when he was killed?"

"Now you're pushing me. The rain doesn't help. It can have a noticeable effect on the temperature of the corpse, and right now that's the only gauge we have for his time of death. Once Dr. Darzi has him on the table, who knows what other indicators he'll find. There was some clotting around the wound, maybe enough to suggest an hour or more, but with the water I really can't tell. You can use all of the cruel cop interrogation methods on me you want, but that's it. That's all I'm going to admit at this point."

Shantel and Clark Macon showed up to take photos and collect whatever evidence the rain hadn't washed away.

"Where's Marcus?" I asked. Marcus Brown was Shantel's regular partner. They'd been a team for years, with Marcus filling in as supervisor any time Shantel was off work.

She gave me a look that I couldn't decipher. Fear, irritation, betrayal, sadness—maybe a mix of all of them. "He's thinking of taking another job," she said flatly. I wasn't sure she was going to say anything else, but then she saw the look of concern on my face.

With a sigh, she explained, "A few months ago, Esther got a job at FAMU's nursing school. You know she'd been working at the nursing home here in town, but she's always wanted to teach. She's been working on her doctorate for years. When she got the job, I knew she wasn't going to be happy living over here and commuting to Tallahassee. For three months she's been on him to move over there and get a job. Apparently, she talked him into applying for a position with FDLE and it looks like he's going to get it. Didn't even tell me he'd put in for the job."

"Family has to come first," I said. It was lame, but the best I could come up with. Shantel and Marcus were good friends and a great team. His leaving would be a blow to all of us.

"He can't refuse her anything." There was more than a little bitterness in her voice, made worse, I was sure, by the fact that Shantel and Esther had been best friends for years. "We'd better get to work," she said, looking around for Clark. They set up lights and hurriedly took pictures. A check of the radar had shown that they only had a small window of opportunity before the next band of rain arrived.

We all helped to collect evidence. Darlene and I pointed out items we thought might be more important than others. The yard had so much junk and trash in it that there would have been no way to collect it all. Besides, Darlene and I were pretty sure that the murderer had never been down in the ditch.

Finally they were finished and I helped Linda and Ann carry the body up the incline to the road. The track was muddy and slippery, but eventually we managed to get the body stowed in the van.

"If you could get us the fingerprints tonight, that would be great," I said to them as they finished packing up.

"That should be doable," Linda said. Fingerprints could be taken electronically and emailed to us, which could mean having his identity nailed down in a few hours.

Julio met back up with us at the cars as the coroner's van and the crime scene van both pulled away. "You're going to be shocked," he said, "but not a single person saw anything. They didn't see someone roll a body down the hill. They didn't see Hitdawg hit the road for parts unknown. Nothin'."

"The body was most likely left after the sun went down. With the weather, most of them are probably telling the truth," I said. The rain started coming down again, with an occasional gust of wind. "I'm going to walk around the neighborhood and see if it looks like anyone has a security camera."

The surrounding neighborhood was lower working class, which had it pluses and minuses when it came to the possibility of security cameras. Camera prices were low enough that most people could afford one if they needed it. In a neighborhood where crime rates were above normal, more than a few people felt the need.

"I'll go north," Darlene said, pulling up the hood on her raincoat as Julio left on another call.

"Maybe we'll have a warrant for Hitdawg's place by the time we've walked the neighborhood," I shouted over the wind and rain.

"I'll keep my fingers crossed," Darlene yelled back.

It would take some luck. Through the miracle of electronics, I'd submitted the warrant to search the house with my phone, though there was very little reason to associate Hitdawg's house with the body. My only rationale for it was our suspicion that the dead man was the person who had robbed the dealer. When I'd walked around the exterior of the house, I'd discovered pry marks on one of the windows. The marks looked old, but I fudged it to make it sound like someone might have broken in recently and therefore we had reason to enter the house to check on the welfare of the people inside, and to ensure that the murderer hadn't entered the dwelling and left evidence.

I found the first camera four houses up and on the other side of the street. It was late, but I didn't want to take the chance of losing the footage, so I pressed the doorbell. Nothing. I knocked loudly and continued to knock until the lights finally came on.

"Who is it? You got the wrong house. Go away," a woman's voice said from the other side of the door.

"Sheriff's office. I'm a deputy," I said, holding my badge up to the peephole.

"You think I'm a fool? Anyone can buy a stupid badge. I don't see no police car out front. Go away."

I held up the ID part of my badge folder.

"I'm Deputy Larry Macklin. There's been a murder up the street and I'm canvassing the neighborhood. I'd like to ask you a few questions."

"Ask away. But I didn't see nothin' and I didn't hear nothin'."

"Would you mind opening the door?"

There was a long pause before the door opened a crack. I could see the chain across the gap.

"You should get something stronger than that chain." I took out my card. "If you call me, I'll be glad to have a deputy come out and do a security assessment of your house. He can recommend upgrades that won't cost too much."

"How do you know what I can and can't afford?" the woman challenged me.

"Look, I noticed you have a security camera on the outside of your house. I'd like to see the footage from this evening."

"That thing doesn't work. My son put it up. He bought an old one and rigged it so the light would glow red like it's working. Who got killed?"

Normally I might have ignored her question, but I felt I owed it to her for getting her out of bed in the middle of the night. "A body was dumped in front of one of the houses by the creek," I told her.

"Why don't you all clean that place up? I bet they got one of those meth houses down there. Lot of nasty business going on in those houses. I've called you all a couple times when I seen trouble."

"We've tried."

"It's the slumlords that own them. That's the trouble. They all need to be torn down." She was getting wound up.

"I couldn't agree more. I'm sorry to bother you. Don't forget to call if you want that security evaluation for your home."

She closed the door and turned off the light.

Two doors down I found another camera. The lights were on in the house and when I knocked on the door, the man that answered it looked almost pleased to see me.

"Hello. What can I do for you?" he said after inspecting my badge. He was a tall, middle-aged black man in a wife-beater shirt and athletic shorts. "Sorry, I was doing my exercises. Hey, I know you! Yeah, I seen that billboard." His face split into a big smile. "Man, oh man, I bet that pissed off your old man. I voted for him the last election, by the way. I knew Grover who was running against him. I wouldn't have trusted him any farther than I could throw him."

"May I come in?"

"Sure, I'm Isaiah," he said, sticking out his hand. He gave me a firm shake before moving back and letting me in.

"I'm here because a body was found down the road. I saw your security camera and was hoping I could look at the footage."

"A body? Crying shame what's happened to this neighborhood. I grew up in this house. My dad had to move to the nursing home last year, so I moved in."

"Good of you to stay," I said.

"This is home," he said, as if that explained everything.

I thought about white people and how a lot of us moved to the most expensive neighborhood we could afford the first chance we got. But in the black community it was often quite different. People would stay in their old neighborhoods even when the neighborhood had problems and they could afford to live somewhere else. Many of these neighborhoods were very close knit, which presented both advantages and disadvantages for law enforcement.

"Can you pull up the footage from your camera?"

"No problem. I got it set up so it runs wireless to my computer." He led me through the small, neat home to a back bedroom that had been turned into an office. The room looked and sounded like a mini version of NASA's mission control, with a dozen computer screens set up around the room and the purr of several large servers.

"I do routing for a couple different companies. Sometimes I even write code for the software they're using so it will do a better job tracking their trucks and shipments. I do a lot of my work at night. The big rush is around seven and eight in the morning, when folks are coming to work and trying to figure out where everything is."

He walked over to a workstation and started to type. Four different camera angles appeared on the screen, showing high-quality images.

"With all my equipment, I wanted to set up a pretty good security system. I've already foiled three crackheads who thought the house would be an easy target," he said. "I've got a camera on the north front corner, south front, north rear and south rear." He pointed out each of the corresponding images. "They're wide angle and cover the entire exterior of the house."

"I'm looking for any cars passing between six and ten tonight."

"So both the front cameras then," Isaiah said, and tapped a key, causing the images of the backyard to disappear from the screen. "The south one covers about halfway across the street so it's not much help with cars going south. You can see that the north camera is at a slightly different angle and would catch most of a car going south. Both of them pick up cars and drivers going north." He rattled this off while he hit keys and the timestamps on both images started to fly backward. He stopped them at five-fifty-six.

The images were taken at half second intervals, causing the video to look glitchy.

"Go ahead and speed it up," I said. I didn't have time to review all of the footage, plus I didn't have a clue what make and model of vehicle I was looking for. And unless the victim appeared in one of the car windows, I didn't have any idea who I was looking for. *Unless it was Klein*, said a voice in my head. But Blake Klein knew all about surveillance cameras. If he was our killer, then I didn't think we would catch him on camera. Tonight, I just wanted to get a sense of the value of the footage.

There were a number of cars and trucks that went by between six and eight. Only after dark did the traffic ease up. The footage was good, but the cameras didn't pick up license tags. It wouldn't really be useful until we had a suspect.

"Can you make a copy for me?" I asked.

"Sure." He grabbed a flash drive from a large bowl of them and inserted it into the computer.

CHAPTER NINE

Ten minutes later, I headed back to my car. Darlene was waiting for me.

"Three cameras, one broken, and two that didn't show the street," she said.

"I got lucky. If our guy came from or headed south, there's a chance we caught him on camera."

"Now we just have to figure out who the bad guy is that's killing other bad guys. What do you think the odds are that it's your buddy Klein?" Darlene asked.

"I can't see it. Maybe I'm just being stubborn. Finding that card on our victim, I have to admit there is some connection. Beyond that, I don't want to speculate."

"You can't discount it."

"Agreed. I'll get some photos of him that we can show to witnesses." Still lacking a warrant for Hitdawg's house, I was getting ready to say that we should both head home when I got a text message. It read: *Call me. No go on the fingerprints. Linda.* I showed Darlene, then called Linda.

"I think you got a real nasty character here," she said. "He's used acid or fire or something to scar up his fingers. I can give you a palm print, but that's all you're going to get. On the other hand, if you lift prints at a scene then it's going to be pretty obvious if they're his."

"He damaged them that bad?"

"I'd have noticed it at the scene if it hadn't been a dark and stormy night," she said, and I could hear the smile in her voice.

"Thanks for the effort," I said and hung up.

"Great! I hate when we don't know who the victim is," Darlene said. She'd been able to hear most of my conversation with Linda.

"Makes coming up with suspects a lot harder. Hey, I've got an idea."

I pulled up a picture of the victim that I'd taken earlier at the scene. I always took a photo of the body to use in witness interviews, but I was usually very careful not to let the picture out of my control. The last thing I wanted to do was to re-victimize families by letting images of their dead loved ones loose on the Internet. In this case, however, I was sure that our victim was not a very lovable character and was willing to take a chance. I sent a close-up of his face to Luke Garner and asked if he recognized our body. I didn't know if Luke turned off his phone when he went to bed or not, but I doubted it.

My instincts were good. My phone rang just seconds later.

"Who is he?" Luke asked, sounding a bit fuzzy-headed.

"That's what we want to know," I said a little testily.

"I mean, why do you think I might know who he is?"

"There might be a connection to Klein."

"Really?" Luke said, sounding much more alert.

"Just a chance. Enough of a chance that I wanted you to take a look at him."

"Okay, I'm looking hard now." His voice sounded farther away and I realized he'd put me on speaker so he could look at the picture and talk at the same time. "What happened to him?"

"All I can tell you is that he was found dead and we have no idea who he is."

"Kind of hard to tell from this picture."

"We just found him this evening. The night was dark and the weather was wet," I said, suddenly feeling how tired I was.

"No, I can't say I recognize him. But I'm dying to know what the connection is between him and Klein. Must be something you found at the scene since you don't know who he is." Luke wasn't dumb.

"I'm going to hold that back for now. Can you look through everything you have on Klein's friends, business associates, family, neighbors, whoever? When we do get this guy's ID, it would help to be able to tie him back to Klein or someone Klein knew."

"Wow! Yep. I'm wide awake now. I was getting up soon anyway. They've issued a voluntary evacuation for the island, but it'll be mandatory in the morning and I was going to get a head start. I was planning to go up to family in Georgia, but I'll head your way instead. I'll bring all my files on Klein and we can go through them." He sounded like a kid going on a camping trip.

"Sure. I'll be staying at the office as part of our emergency management team. You can meet me there," I said. Truth was, it would give me something to do while I was sitting around waiting for an emergency to manage.

"Cool. See you tomorrow!" He hung up and I imagined him doing a jig of happiness at the fact his suspicions were being proved true.

"You boys are going to have quite the sleepover," Darlene said. I just glared at her.

All the way home, I wrestled with myself. I had to tell Cara what I'd done after I'd thought that Klein had been killed. The sooner the better, but I was afraid she wouldn't take the news well and discussing it with her at three in the morning seemed insane. But if not now, then when? With the storm coming, I might not have another chance for days. Besides,

I'd already tipped my hand with my earlier phone call. She was going to want to know why I had suddenly become so paranoid. And if there was real danger, then she needed to know as much as possible so she could be on her guard. Like it or not, I had to tell her.

I stopped in the driveway to open the metal farm gate that blocked the road onto our twenty acres. On most nights when I came home this late, I just left it open, but tonight I made sure to close and lock it behind me.

The kitchen light was on in the house. As soon as I got out of the car, I saw Cara peering out the window. She opened the door for me and a gust of wind almost blew it out of her hand.

"Getting a little blustery," I said as I kissed her.

"What's wrong?" she asked immediately.

"Let's go sit down," I said, taking her hand and leading her over to the couch.

"What?" Cara asked, her eyes worried.

"Remember our week at Pelican Island? Everything that Blake Klein was suspected of doing?"

"Murder, blackmail, a bunch of stuff. What's going on?"

"There's a chance he might still be alive," I said bluntly.

"But you and your dad saw his boat crash."

"Yes, we did. But like I told you, the Coast Guard never found a body, so we can't be one hundred percent sure. That suicide Luke asked me to take a look at... there is some evidence it might be tied to Klein. And tonight's gunshot victim also appears to have some link to him."

"That's awful." I watched her eyes grow wide as she thought it through. "You think he might come after you and your dad?"

"That's part of it." I didn't know how to tell her the rest.

"What else?"

"You know how Klein used hidden cameras to blackmail people who bought the houses he sold?" I asked, pausing to let it sink in.

"You didn't give me a lot of details, but yeah..."

"The house we were staying in was one of those houses."

"Are you saying…"

"I don't know how much was recorded. All I know is that I found a camera in the room we slept in," I said.

"And you didn't tell me?"

"Klein was killed right after I found the camera. At least, I *thought* he was killed."

"Now you're saying there could be video of us…" I saw darkness come into her eyes.

"I found the place where Klein kept his recordings, even his backup servers. I destroyed all of it. Not just for our sakes, but for everyone involved. He hurt a bunch of people. I just wanted to make sure that no one else could ever be victimized by Blake Klein."

"But you should have told me," Cara said angrily.

"I didn't want you to have to worry about something that I had taken care of."

"I had a right to know what had been done to us… to me."

"I guess. But I didn't think you should have to worry about it. Besides, I broke the law when I destroyed that evidence. There was no point in making you an accessory to a felony."

"You're making my point! Those were huge decisions. I should have been allowed to make those decisions for myself." She was tense and trembling.

"I was willing to take my chances in order to protect you," I said, feeling hurt that she didn't seem to appreciate the huge risk I had taken for her.

"What happens to you happens to me. I might have been willing to take a chance on those videos getting out rather than have you risk your job and your freedom to destroy them."

"Would you have really done that? Would you have wanted to take that chance?" I shot back.

"I don't know. But you didn't let me decide, did you?" She got up and walked into the kitchen.

"I made the decision I thought was right," I said lamely to her back.

She poured herself a glass of water and drank it before turning back to me. "We both need to get some sleep," she muttered.

"I know that you're mad and there's nothing I can do right now to make you feel better."

"Don't," Cara said, shaking her head.

"Do you want me to sleep out here?" I asked.

Her eyes softened for a moment. "No."

I still wasn't sure if I had screwed up as badly as she obviously thought I had. Selfishly, I wanted some sign from her that we'd get through this, but I let it go. I couldn't press her.

We lay side by side in bed for a while, a palpable tension between us. Finally, Cara reached out and touched my hand lightly for a second before rolling over. Deciding to take it as a small olive branch, I rolled the other way and tried to sleep.

I was up by six and my phone was buzzing regularly with incoming text messages. Most of them were emergency management team alerts. Cara's phone was lighting up as well. She was already in the shower with the door closed.

After sending Dad a text with my ETA, I ate breakfast and petted Ivy while I waited for Cara to finish up. Poor Alvin was lying on the floor where he could see both me and past me into the bedroom. His scrunched-up face looked as depressed as I was feeling.

"What's up, little guy? Are you picking up on the bad vibes?" His eyes shifted to me for a second and then went back to the bedroom doorway. "I've got some bad news for both of you. You're going be playing house with your Uncle Mauser." As I said it, I realized I should probably get some things ready for them.

I packed a bag of food and other supplies to send with them to Dad's. *Better be my most useful self*, I thought.

When Cara came out, we discussed Alvin and Ivy.

"According to the current forecast, I should be able come home and take them to your dad's this afternoon before we start getting the worst of the wind," Cara offered, after checking the National Hurricane Center's tracking map.

"If you can't make it, then I should be able to," I said.

"What about the house?" Cara asked, looking around nervously.

"There's not much we can do. Unless one of the trees falls on it, it should be fine. We'll lose power, but we don't have to worry about flooding."

She let me pull her into a quick hug. "It will all be fine," I reassured her.

We took both cars. When I got to the gate, I opened it for her and let her through before closing and locking the gate behind me. The sky was angry with dark and swirling clouds, but for the moment there was no rain and little wind.

"Larry!" a voice shouted. My hand flew to my gun. "Hey, I didn't mean to startle you."

I turned and saw Mr. Herman, one of my neighbors.

"Sorry! You made me jump," I said. "I'm surprised you're out walking this morning."

Mr. Herman was in his seventies and walked with a noticeable hitch, which looked more pronounced this morning.

"I got a new knee last month. Doctor said to walk as much as possible to break it in. I figured this was my last chance to get out and give it a good go for a couple of days."

"You all got everything you need?"

"Water, generator, gas. We're good. How 'bout you? They got you working?"

"Emergency management," I said, and he nodded sagely.

"Caught any critters on your game cam?" he asked, and I stared at him like I didn't have a clue what he was talking about because, frankly, I didn't.

"What?"

"Your fancy new game cam," he said, pointing off to the

side of the road.

I'd used game cameras in the past when I wanted to watch my gate, but I didn't have any in place now. I followed his finger and finally saw, about twenty feet off of my drive, a small, well-camouflaged video camera.

"Thanks," I said, giving Mr. Herman a brief wave. He stared at me oddly. "I think someone is playing a joke on me," I added, trying to sound light-hearted.

Mr. Herman nodded and smiled, then continued on his walk.

I went to my trunk, grabbed an evidence bag and pulled on some gloves. I walked over to the camera and examined it carefully, taking a few pictures with my phone before removing the straps that held it to the pine tree. This wasn't an ordinary game cam. From what I could tell, it looked like someone had taken a regular game camera apart and reassembled the pieces into a more compact, sealed unit. Since there didn't seem to be any way to get a memory card into or out of it, I decided that it must have uploaded its images wirelessly. It was weird and disconcerting. I hoped Lionel would be in the office.

Placing the camera in the evidence bag, I carried it to my car and put it in the trunk. I handled it as gingerly as if it had been a bomb. For a second, I wondered if it was possible that it *did* contain an explosive, but I immediately dismissed the idea. If it was an IED, then I would have already lost a hand or worse.

Are there any other cameras on my property? I asked myself as I headed in to the office.

When I got to my desk, I saw Darlene wrestling with Mauser. The big goof was jumping back excitedly and then charging at Darlene, who flailed her arms around playfully.

"Why are you playing nice with her?" I asked Mauser. "If that was me, you'd be jumping on top of me."

"I'm not his big brother," Darlene said without looking up.

"What are you doing with the monster anyway?" I asked,

and looked around to see if my dad was lurking anywhere in CID. "For that matter, why is he even here today?"

"Your dad said Genie's running some last-minute errands, and the dogsitter's not coming until the afternoon. So he asked me to look after Mauser while he went over to the emergency management center."

"You should file a complaint. Dog-sitting is not part of the duties of an Adams County deputy."

"Don't be such a sourpuss," she said, and redoubled her game with Mauser.

"When are you heading over to the elementary school?" Most personnel from CID were being stationed at the closest emergency shelter to our office.

"I'm actually on duty at the high school."

"I thought CID was going to be at Adams Elementary."

"Most of them are. I just happened to get assigned to the shelter at the high school."

A light dawned. "Oh, wait. You *traded* for a spot at the high school, didn't you?"

"Maybe," she said, as Mauser upped the energy level and rammed into her while trying to grab one of her hands with his mouth.

"Let me guess. Hondo is stationed at the high school." Hondo, whose real name was Alejandro Valdez, was Darlene's new beau. He was a senior paramedic with Adams County EMS.

"Smarty pants. You're going to have your girl just across the street, so don't be pointing fingers."

"No finger-pointing here." I held up my hands in a gesture of surrender, which Mauser took to mean that I was joining in the game. He bounced over to me and attempted to climb in my lap. "Not going to happen, you bone-headed monster."

The words were barely out of my mouth before he jumped up and slammed his head against mine. Hard. "Son of a…" I said, gritting my teeth.

"Bet that hurt," Darlene said, trying to control her

laughter. "Now how do you ever expect us to have a viral video if you don't tell me before you do something stupid?"

I held up my middle finger while trying to shake off the pain. When I stopped seeing stars, I looked down to see Mauser sitting in front of me, looking like an innocent man on death row.

"I don't guess you even felt that?" He just blinked at me. "Didn't think so."

I heard a loud banging and turned to see Charley Wright and one of his assistants outside putting plywood over the windows.

"I checked with dispatch, but there hasn't been any word on Hitdawg," Darlene said.

"We need to get the names of all the dealers and addicts that were robbed by our victim. All of them need to be on our suspect list." I reached up and gently touched the place on my forehead where I could already feel a lump. "You're a menace," I told Mauser, who was now flopped on his side pretending to be asleep.

I looked down at my phone and wondered how long it would take Luke to get there. Then I dumped the evidence bag with the game camera onto Darlene's desk. "This is something else that might or might not be related."

She picked up the bag and looked at the camera. "This is a custom job. Where'd you find it?"

I told her about my encounter with Mr. Herman and the discovery of the camera.

"Looks like you've got a stalker. Wait, didn't Klein use hidden cameras as part of his shtick?"

"Yep."

"Layers and layers of old Mister Onion," she said.

"I'm going to take it to Shantel first, and then to Lionel when she gets done fingerprinting it. Wanna come?"

"I don't think Shantel is going to want the big blue ox in her china shop," Darlene said, nodding at Mauser.

Just then, Pete waltzed into CID.

"You look too happy for the current weather

conditions," I told him.

"I'm as happy as the only kid on the block with a full-size house generator when there's a hurricane bearing down. I bought that sucker last year and had to listen to Sarah complain about it all winter when she wanted to park her car in the garage. All I'm asking for is a day without power. That happens and I'm proven right." He clapped his hands together gleefully.

"You'd leave your neighborhood in darkness just to prove to your wife that buying a two-hundred-pound generator was a smart move?"

"Damn right," he said, and then squinted at me. "Hey, who clobbered you in the forehead?"

I pointed to Mauser, who was still playing the part of the innocent. "Speaking of which, would you mind watching him while we go down to see Shantel?"

"No problem. Anyone who hits you in the head is a friend of mine," Pete said, causing Mauser to raise his head and look at him as if he'd understood what he was saying.

Darlene followed me down to the evidence room, where Shantel was busy locking things up.

"I'm putting a seal on everything in the office. The stuff in the vault should be all right. Marcus and I are the only ones with the combination." She pointed to the large walk-in closet in the back of her office. Everyone referred to it as the vault, though it was really just a large, windowless room with reinforced concrete walls and a vault door. The room held a variety of evidence dating back a decade or more. There were enough drugs in the room to keep the whole county high for years.

"I can't believe you don't even trust me with the combination," I said with a smile.

The vault was one of the first upgrades Dad had made when he became sheriff. Then he'd let everyone know that there would be one key person and one backup who would be responsible for all the evidence inside. Too many law enforcement offices had had drugs and money walk out of their evidence rooms.

"I don't know who's going to back me up when Marcus leaves," Shantel said, her face clouding up.

"Is it a sure thing?"

"He says he hasn't made up his mind, but he'll never stand up to Esther."

The look on Shantel's face told me that losing Marcus would be as hard for her as any break up or a death in the family. We form strong attachments to the people we work with, even more so when it's a high-stress job that demands teamwork.

"If you've got a moment, I'd appreciate you processing this." I held up the evidence bag with the camera in it. I thought she might give me a snarky comeback, but a few months ago I'd helped find her missing niece and, ever since, she'd given my requests priority. I'd made it a point not to take too much advantage of her goodwill.

"What the heck is it?" Shantel asked, eyeing the bag suspiciously as she took it from me.

She gloved up, took the camera out of the bag and began working over it with all of her lights, powders and magic for picking up fingerprints. Finding nothing but a few smudges on the outside, she got her camera and took pictures of all sides of the game cam before grabbing a screwdriver.

"I'm going to open it up," she said, poised with the screwdriver.

"Wait!" I said dramatically. "Let me see if Lionel is available."

Five minutes later, Lionel was standing with us as Shantel unscrewed the outer casing of the camera. We must have looked like a group of doctors hovering over a patient.

"No chance this thing is going to explode, is there?" Shantel suddenly asked, echoing my earlier concerns.

"Probably not," I said, and then thought better of it. "But it might not be a bad idea for all of us to put on goggles."

There was another interval, then we were all giving the camera a bug-eyed stare. I think we held our collective breath when Shantel got the fourth screw out and pulled the two halves apart. The inside of the box looked like the inner workings of a bomb, but it was soon clear that it was nothing more than the souped-up camera I thought it was.

"See that?" Lionel pointed to what looked like a miscellaneous electronic part. "That's for wifi. Someone can be within, say, ten feet with a cell phone acting as a personal hotspot and upload everything from the camera. Interesting."

"It's using some high-end batteries too," I said, pointing to four lithium batteries.

"Here's something," Shantel said. Reaching for an evidence bag, she gently shook the case and a small amount of sand fell out into the bag.

"This is Florida. There's sand everywhere," Darlene said.

"If you get lucky, this sand might have something a bit unusual in it. I read an article a couple months ago where sand in a shoe was used to prove that a suspect had been to the same beach where the victim had been abducted."

"Would tell us something if this sand is from the beach," I mused.

"Specifically the beaches on Pelican Island," Darlene agreed.

My mind was screaming that there was something wrong with all of this. Two seemingly unconnected dead bodies and the spy camera. How did they add up? Of course, the very thought that Blake Klein was still walking around free was enough to put me on edge.

"There's an SD memory card," Lionel said, pointing to a little bit of red sticking out of a slot in the camera's inner workings.

Shantel took some tweezers from her kit and pulled it out. When Lionel reached out like he was going to grab it, she slapped his hand. "Back up. I haven't fingerprinted it," she told him.

When she was done, she put the card in an evidence bag, assigned it a number and took a picture of it in the bag before handing it over to Lionel.

"Is there any way to identify the phone that was used as a personal hotspot?" I asked Lionel.

"Maybe. Of course, it might not be a phone. You can buy portable units that even come with battery packs. Thinking like a criminal, that would make more sense than using a phone. Less chance of leaving an electronic fingerprint."

"Great. Better mousetraps followed by better mice," I grumbled.

"It's the great wheel of life," Darlene said with a wink.

"You okay with me taking the rest of it apart to look for fingerprints?" Shantel asked.

"You got what you need?" I asked Lionel.

"I'll need that part," he said, pointing to the small object with the slot for the memory card.

"I can take that out next," Shantel said.

Darlene and I left them to their electronic autopsy.

"This stupid hurricane. I need to find out who's behind all of this, but everything is going to be on lock-down soon."

"You have to consider that the camera isn't even related to last night's murder," Darlene said as we made our way back to CID. The building was getting darker inside as Charley and company continued boarding up the windows.

"I know. I can't even be sure that the first body was a suicide or a homicide, let alone whether it's connected to the second murder. Then you throw in the camera. Nothing about this makes me feel good."

"We'll figure it all out," Darlene said, channeling her inner nurturer.

CHAPTER TEN

Pete was at his desk, working on reports and eating an apple. Mauser was nowhere to be seen.

"Where's Mauser?" I asked.

"Who?" Pete said.

"The floppy-eared moose," Darlene said.

"Oh, him. The other guy from the billboard came in and got him."

"I really don't like it when you're in this good of a mood," I told him.

"That's exactly what Sarah says. You all could give me a complex."

"I'm going to give you some Xanax," I said.

"Did I hear right? You guys found your robber dead at one of the houses in the Ditch?" Pete asked, his tone more serious.

"Yep. Someone shot him and rolled him down the hill in front of Hitdawg's house."

Pete reached into a stack of papers on his desk. "This probably goes with your cases. It's a report I took when we divvied things up a couple days ago. Remember the purse-snatching? Wasn't exactly a purse-snatching. I went to interview the victim and turns out it was Baggie."

Darlene and I both raised our eyebrows. Katie Burke had gotten her nickname the first time she was pulled in for dealing crack. She'd been found holding dozens of small jewel bags used for distributing drugs. Of course, she'd also been found with a good amount of crack and a thousand dollars and change. But when she was brought in, all she did was yell out asking if it was against the law to have baggies. That was the only thing she would admit to, even though two deputies had been present when the drugs and money were found in pockets she had sewn into her clothes. Forevermore, she was known as Baggie.

"Let me guess. She was robbed at gunpoint."

"Hole in one. To her credit, she didn't report it. Baggie is smarter than that. It was her mother, who's a few bricks short of a load, who called it in. After talking to her mother, I think she actually wanted me to arrest Baggie."

He held out the report and I took it.

"That's Deputy Spears's original report. I'm just finishing up my follow-up. I'll send it to you when I'm done. I'll also gladly email Lt. Johnson and tell him I've lobbed the ball into your court."

"Wow. You're just having a wonderful day," I said with narrowed eyes.

"Sometimes you get the bear, sometimes the bear gets you."

I read over the report, then turned to Darlene. "I'm going to talk to Baggie."

"I'll ride along."

"How well do you know her?"

"Pretty well. When I worked with the city, I had to deal with her on a regular basis. She thought she could use me as her personal enforcer. Baggie never learned. She'd call me up and complain whenever some other dealer was trying to take her corner away. Of course, she didn't exactly put it that way. She'd say that some guy was giving her the eye or making rude comments to her. And it was all true. But what she failed to mention was that she had tried to stab the guy for selling on her corner, or she'd tried to set his customers on fire. Baggie is a real piece of work."

"She's been selling on the streets for a while. Baggie's been a legend since before I started working as a deputy."

"She started when she was fourteen, maybe fifteen? Sad world," Darlene said.

The rain was coming down in sheets when we got to the door.

"My car. It's closest," I said.

"Go ahead and press the unlock button now. I bet I can beat you there."

"I could get the car and pick you up," I offered.

"You wish, turtle boy." She stepped out and stood on the sidewalk under the eaves. "On the count of three."

"This is childish," I said, having to shout to be heard over the rain.

"That's what losers always say. One."

"Two."

"Three!" and she was off running through the rain. I caught up with her and got to my side of the car first, but fumbled the latch.

"Ho, ho. Inside with the door closed first," she gloated.

"My door was farther away," I said.

"You did okay for a punk kid." She shook some of the water off herself. "You ever watch any of those noir mysteries?"

"A little. We've seen that Scandinavian one with Kenneth Branagh."

"Perfect example! Everyone is always moping around in that show. If I didn't have some fun at this job, I'd quit and find something else to do. Life's too short."

"When we first became partners, I thought I was going to have to quit," I joked.

"You just got your panties in a wad 'cause I tried to arrest you. Good times."

"I don't think this Hondo thing is good for you. Makes you too happy," I said, trying to see where I was going through all the rain as I pulled out onto the road. We were a block off of Calhoun's main north-south drag, and I could see the cars lined up bumper-to-bumper, going north to escape the storm.

"You'd have to drive a long way to find a hotel room tonight," Darlene said.

We pulled up in front of Mrs. Burke's house, where Baggie was temporarily hiding out. A knock on the door summoned a middle-aged woman who couldn't have been five feet tall if she stood on tiptoes. She wore a pants suit that was a size or two too small for her plus-size figure. I wouldn't have dared venture a guess as to what her original hair color had been. Currently, it was a strange yellow-orange that drew attention to her pale white skin.

"Mrs. Burke?" I asked. I'd never met Baggie's mother.

"Cops. Yeah, I'm Katie's mother. Come on in out of the storm. Gonna get worse 'for it gets better." She dug into her pocket, pulled out a cigarette and lit it. "Sit down somewhere. I'll go get her."

Mrs. Burke took two steps toward the back of the small house and screamed for Katie to get up and come talk to the damn police.

"You need to catch this guy who put a gun in my baby's face," she said, pointing the cigarette at us.

Darlene and I were both standing in front of the sofa. It was never a good idea to get too settled before your witness-slash-suspect-slash-whatever had made an appearance.

Baggie came stumbling out of the back of the house. She was in her late twenties, but still dressed like a fifteen year-old. Her eyes were blurry and her dirty blonde hair looked like it hadn't been combed in a week. She was almost a foot taller than her mother.

"You better catch him," her mother repeated. "'Cause I got to get her out of my house. She got scared to damn death and won't hardly go outside."

"Hush, Momma, they don't care about that," she said, not looking at her mother. "Believe me, I want out of here as bad as you want me out. But not with that crazy man out there. I ain't never had problems with nobody where I get a damn gun shoved in my face. I mean, what the hell? Momma's right, you need to catch that crazy man. I see him again, I'm going to pop him." She mimed shooting someone with her finger.

"Funny you should say that, darlin'. 'Cause we found the man last night with a bullet hole in his head," Darlene said.

Neither one of us believed that Baggie had it in her to shoot someone in cold blood. Probably not even in hot blood. Darlene just wanted to see Baggie's face and it was worth it. Her mouth fell open and stayed open while her eyes grew to the size of half dollars.

"I knew someone would shoot him. You can't go around robbing folks like that." By folks, of course, she meant drug dealers and addicts. "Didn't I tell you, Momma?"

"Great. I'll go pack up your stuff," her mother said. I thought it was a joke until she turned and headed for the back of the house.

"We want you to tell us about the robbery," I said.

"You ain't going to arrest me for nothing, right?" Baggie asked.

"We *can't* arrest you. The clerk told us they don't have any more room in your file," Darlene told her.

Baggie narrowed her eyes and stared at Darlene, trying to decide if that could possibly be true. "I'm serious now," she said after dismissing the notion.

"No. You are a victim in this case. We want you to be candid with us," I assured her.

"Yeah, okay. 'Cause he was a real asshole." Her face took on an odd mix of fear, betrayal and anger.

"This can't be the first time you've been robbed."

"Noooo. I've been robbed a lot. A whole lot. Just... Never like this. He... I really thought he might shoot me. I ain't never had someone look at me like that," Baggie said. "I've been hit and everything. Keshone beat the crap out of me a lot. But I don't know... Nothing like that guy." She sounded surprised at her own fear. "You sure he's dead?"

"The body we have is definitely dead. We're pretty sure that it's the same guy who's been robbing people at gunpoint," I said.

"You mean there's a chance it ain't the guy? Momma, quit packing my stuff!" she said with an ear-piercing shriek.

"We're hoping you can help us determine if this is the guy that robbed you," I said, realizing there was a slim chance it *wasn't* the same guy. Could the robber have killed someone else, dressed him in his clothes and left him at the scene of one of the robberies in order to throw us off his trail? It was possible.

"He was wearing a mask, gloves and all black clothes," Baggie blurted.

"Slow down. We read the report, but we'd like to hear you tell the whole story from the beginning," Darlene said.

Baggie sighed dramatically. "Okay, fine. I was at my regular place on the porch of the house at Gordon and King Streets. And everything was fine. My regulars were coming by."

"This was Sunday night?"

"Yeah. Sunday is a good night."

"Why'd you wait a couple of days to report it?"

"I didn't report nothin'. Momma reported it after I moved back into my old room. She started screaming at me that I couldn't stay. I told her I was scared of this guy. Then she screwed me over by reporting it to the police."

"I can hear you!" her mother yelled from the back of the house. "I had to report you. I can't have you staying here and doing all your crazy stuff in my house. I'm not going to get in trouble 'cause you're so stupid."

"Shut up!" Baggie yelled. "See, that's why I turned out the way I did."

"Liar! You turned out to be a drug dealer 'cause you never listened to me and you're lazy as sin," her mother shouted back.

"I said, quit packing my stuff! The dead guy might not be

the same asshole that pointed a gun at me."

"Okay, so you were at the crack house at Gordon and King selling drugs to people who came by," Darlene said, trying to get the interview back on track.

Baggie frowned. "I didn't say I was selling no drugs," she said forcefully.

"Fine. You were handing out lollipops. What happened next?"

"I know you, Deputy Darlene, and I don't like you much," she said grumpily

"You're breaking my heart. I sincerely apologize for suggesting that you might be engaged in any illegal activity. Please go on." The snark was deep.

"What time was this?" I cut in.

"Dark. I don't know. Maybe ten o'clock. I still had plenty of… never mind."

"Roughly ten. Go on," I prompted.

"There was a point when it was just Tattoo and me."

"Who's Tattoo?" This was the first we'd heard about this. No one else had been mentioned in the report.

"He's a kid who keeps me company," she said warily.

"I promised we wouldn't arrest you. However, if I ever catch you using an underage kid to hold drugs for you, then I will take you in and make sure the charges stick. Do you understand me?" I told her. It was one thing for her to be living the gutter lifestyle, but it was quite another to be using an underage kid as a go-between to avoid charges.

"Do you want to hear about the robbery or not?" she said. "I sent Tattoo home 'cause it was late. See, I'm taking care of the kid. Anyway, not long after he leaves, I hear this noise in the bushes. Not like sneaky, but more like someone is just falling around in them. I figure it's some meth head, so I wasn't worried. But then, like all of a sudden, this guy is on the other side of me, growling at me to give him all my money and… other stuff. He was holding his gun out at me like he was used to shooting people. He wasn't shaking or nothin'. I told him I got my stuff from… I told him who and said robbing me would piss him off. The guy just laughed. Like he wasn't scared of nobody. Not like a person who's high ain't scared. This guy wasn't high; he was real straight. Even under the mask, I could see him smile. That's when I peed myself. I'm serious. I let loose. I just knew he was going to pull the trigger." She stopped and I could tell by the look in eyes that she was reliving the fear.

"What type of gun did he use?" I asked.

"Big, black. I don't know. I don't do guns."

"How did he take the money and drugs? Did he have a bag to put them in?"

"Yeah, I forgot that. He threw a pillowcase at me. Told me to fill it up."

"Think. Did you see a watch or notice anything about his shoes?" Darlene said.

"His jeans. Black jeans and they fit real tight around his ass. A real bubble butt, you know?"

"You were scared to death and yet you noticed his ass?" I asked.

"I can't help it. Kind of weird, I know, but I was thinking I'm gonna die, but he sure has a nice butt."

"I can't believe you're my daughter!" came another shout from the back of the house.

"Shut up!" she screamed back.

My head hadn't recovered from the knock I got from Mauser and all this shouting wasn't helping. I rubbed my temples in irritation.

"That's all you can remember from the attack?" Darlene asked, sounding as disgusted as I felt.

"He was pointing that gun at me. What was I supposed to notice?"

"Besides his ass?"

"Hey, I told you about it, didn't I?"

"You did do that," I said, deciding that we'd gotten all we could from her. "If you think of anything else, call us. Your assistance will be taken into consideration if… when you get in trouble in the future. Understand?" I said over the throbbing in my head.

"Yeah, okay. You know, I saw him yesterday," Baggie said, causing my head to snap around and Darlene's jaw to hit the floor.

"What?" I couldn't believe she hadn't mentioned this until now.

"Yeah, down by the police station."

"On the square?" I asked, thinking she was referring to the Calhoun Police Department's small station across from the courthouse.

"Nah, your station."

"The sheriff's office?"

"Yeah, near there."

"He was wearing his mask?"

"No. Just his jeans and a blue T-shirt."

"How did you know it was him?" I asked, afraid that I already knew the answer.

"I saw his butt in those jeans. Same jeans, same ass," she said, pleased with herself.

I took a deep breath and tried to decide how much I trusted her butt recognition system.

"You saw his ass and knew it was him. So then you saw his face, right?" Darlene asked.

"Well, yeah. He wasn't bad looking. Kind of dark like. Dark hair, kind of a hairy face."

"He had a beard?"

"No, just grizzly. You know, unshaven, but not a beard or mustache or anything."

"Where were you when you saw him?"

"I was in Mom's car. We were waiting at the light."

"Let me get this straight. You made a report that a man robbed you at gunpoint. You see the same guy standing outside the sheriff's office a day or so later and yet you didn't bother to let a deputy know this?" I was stunned. Having dealt with plenty of drug dealers and addicts of all descriptions, I understood that they didn't think the same way as the rest of us. They had a different set of rules they followed. However, this seemed a bit extreme.

"I never wanted to make that report in the first place. Besides, when I saw him I got scared all over again." Her voice had the tremor of a frightened child.

"Okay." I held up my hand. "I'll give you a pass on that." I took out my phone and brought up the picture of our victim. "Do you recognize this man?" I showed her the close-up of his pale face, wet from the rain.

"That's him!" she said and stared at the phone. I started to take it back, but she reached out and held it, looking hard at the image of the dead man. "Creepy."

I hadn't seen her mother come into the room. She was holding a large handbag and a backpack that had seen better days.

"You can go back to your apartment if he's dead," Mrs. Burke said firmly.

"And glad to."

"We'll drop you off, but you have to show us where you saw this guy," I said.

"Yeah, sure, okay." Baggie got up and, stomping her feet like a grumpy ten-year-old, she said to her mother, "I'm taking my food too."

"Be my guest. I don't want all your junk in my refrigerator anyway," Mrs. Burke responded.

When Baggie was in the kitchen banging cabinet doors, her mother moved over next to me. "Could you help Katie the way you helped Eddie?" Her question and tone took me by surprise.

"You know Eddie Thompson?"

"Oh, yeah. He used to hang out with Katie when he was using. They'd come by here on a bender. The next morning, he'd be asleep on my couch. Not like the others, though. He was always very polite when he was sober. Sometimes he'd even do a few chores around here before taking off. I seen him a few times since he got clean. He told me you helped him a lot. Katie just needs a helping hand. Someone to get her started."

"Has she been through a rehab program?" I had a vague idea how many times she'd been to court. I couldn't believe she hadn't been sent to a program at some point.

"Yeah, but she never sticks to it. She needs someone to, you know, be her friend. Encourage her. She never has listened to me." She shook her head sadly.

"Eddie got clean on his own. Katie would have to want to get clean." I emphasized the word "want." When I saw the woman's shoulders droop, I added, "I'll have a word with her."

Darlene looked at me with a smirk on her face. I knew she was thinking I was a sucker.

Baggie came out of the kitchen carrying two plastic grocery bags stuffed to the brim with junk food and Cokes. I reached out and took her backpack and handbag.

The rain was still coming down, forcing us to quickstep to the car. When we were all in, I pulled out into the street and headed back toward the office.

As I came close to the office I slowed down, which pissed off the drivers behind me, many of whom had been fighting the rain and other evacuees for hours to escape the coming storm.

"Okay, Katie, where did you see this guy?" Darlene asked her.

Through the rearview mirror, I watched as Baggie moved over in her seat and looked closely. But she was looking out her window toward the jail, not the sheriff's office.

"He was over there in that parking lot. He was looking around. I was afraid he'd see me," she said.

"So he was in front of the jail, not the sheriff's office?" Darlene said.

"Yeah, whatever. But that's where I saw him." Baggie sounded sure.

Did he have a friend in the jail? I wondered. Birds of a feather and all that.

We took Baggie to her duplex, which was only a couple of blocks from the Ditch. I pulled up in front of her unit, then turned around to look at her. "By the way, do you know Hitdawg?"

"Why?"

"Just answer the question."

"Sure, I know him."

"We'd like to talk to him. Do you know where he is?"

"I've been hiding out at Mom's. How the hell would I know?"

"Maybe you texted him or called him," Darlene suggested.

"We ain't on texting terms," she said. *Rivals in the dealing business*, I thought.

"If you bump into him, tell him we want to talk. We don't see him as the killer, but it will go easier if he comes in to see us," Darlene said.

"Yeah, sure." She reached for the door handle.

With a sigh, I opened my own door. "I'll help you into the house," I offered and heard Darlene guffaw.

"Your mom wants you to get clean," I said when we were under the awning in front of her door.

"She thinks I'm like some meth head. I don't use that much. Can't sell and be an addict," Baggie said, and I knew she was right. Some people were able to just sample the products they sold.

"You know, if you get picked up and hit with a serious charge, the judge isn't going to have a choice. You rack up enough points and you'll find yourself locked up for life."

"I know," she said, holding onto the door knob. "I'll be all right." She opened the door and dragged her stuff inside.

CHAPTER ELEVEN

When I got back in the car, Darlene gave me a look and a shake of her head. "Eddie is one thing. Baggie is quite another."

"I just warned her that she can't go on like this forever."

"You shouldn't get attached."

"Do you think she really saw him?" I asked to change the subject.

"To my surprise, I do. It's strange. He was a predator, but now he's in our morgue. So who are we chasing?"

"A super predator," I answered, and thought that was exactly how I'd describe Blake Klein.

"Cases like this are hard 'cause it's so easy to get distracted."

"Keep to the basics. Motive. Why was he killed?"

"For money. He was robbing people of their dope and money. Along comes a bigger fish and robs him."

"Makes sense."

"*There's* someone with the right idea," she said, pointing to a small SUV with a canoe strapped to its roof that was parked in the jail's lot across the street from the sheriff's office.

"You could do some whitewater canoeing through the

parking lot," I said, watching the small river running down the side of the road toward a storm drain.

I parked the car outside the sheriff's office, but it was raining even harder now, with buckets of water pounding the roof. Neither of us made a move to get out. "Or it could be revenge. He hit the wrong bad guy," I suggested.

"You go around stealing honey from the bees, sooner or later you're going to get stung. If the Thompsons were still running things, I'd put my money on them. But right now, we don't have any big fish operating in the county."

"Not that I know of. It would take just the right guy to get the drop on a character like this."

"Agreed. Revenge is a possible motive."

"Why drop him off at Hitdawg's house?"

"To make a statement. But what's the statement?"

"Maybe whoever had it out for our victim also had a grudge against Hitdawg," I said thoughtfully.

"The killer was definitely trying to communicate something to somebody. Otherwise you'd just dump the body out in the woods."

"Or leave it where it fell. These days you're taking a big chance putting a body in your car."

"With all the true crime TV shows out there, even the dumbest criminal knows that."

"Might help if we knew why he was standing out in front of the jail."

"Maybe had a friend who was getting out." Darlene echoed my earlier thought. "I'll check and see if they released anyone around that time."

"Knowing who he is would help too. Since he went to the trouble to destroy his fingerprints, I think there is a good chance he's been in prison and didn't want his prints matched up."

"Makes sense. Maybe he even escaped from prison."

"Either way, let's circulate his picture to all the prisons in the state. See if we can't send it to ones in Alabama and Georgia too."

"DNA will answer that question."

"I don't want to wait a month or more."

"Especially if he's tied to your stalker problem," Darlene agreed. "Maybe you're in luck and he *was* your stalker."

"Why? I certainly don't recognize him."

"Maybe he was working for Klein."

"I thought about that, but I'm not sure. He put up the cameras at my place and came by and uploaded the images every couple of nights, and when he was bored he went out robbing drug dealers for fun and profit." Even as I said it, I couldn't see the sense in it.

"He hits the wrong person and gets killed," Darlene said.

"That part of it I can buy." My phone buzzed with a text update for the storm. "Looks like it's still on track to make landfall to our west sometime early tomorrow morning,"

"Right side of the storm is the worst," Darlene said. "We better wrap up what we're doing. I need to get over to the high school."

"I just bet you do."

"Funny boy."

"Are you coming in or do you want me to drive you over to your car?" With all the construction equipment and fencing set up in the parking lot, I could save Darlene from getting completely soaked by driving my car over to where hers was parked on the back side of the building.

"That would be good," she agreed.

I parked as close to her car as I could without making it impossible to open the doors.

"We'll get back on the investigation as soon as the storm passes," she promised before hopping out of my car and into hers.

I pulled out my phone and texted Cara to find out where she was. We'd agreed that she would go home and take Alvin and Ivy to Dad's before getting locked down at the emergency management center, but I didn't want her to be at the house alone until we'd figured out who was spying on us. After last night, I wasn't looking forward to bringing up

Klein and hidden cameras again.

She responded that she was still at the clinic, so I told her I was headed her way. With Cara already irritated with me, I didn't want to discuss something as unnerving as a stalker over the phone.

Before I drove off, I looked at the parking lot. Where was Luke? I called him.

"Traffic is moving at a snail's pace. I can't help but think that the hurricane is moving faster than we are," he said. His usual *bonhomie* and good humor didn't seem up to the bumper-to-bumper traffic coming from the coast. "I'm only about twenty miles away now, so I should get there sometime next week."

"Good luck. I'll see you when you get here," I told him and headed to Dr. Barnhill's clinic.

The parking lot was full and inside was organized chaos. Some of the people in the lobby were regular clients who were worried there was something wrong with their animals and didn't want to take a chance of not being able to get veterinary care during the storm. Others were there to drop off their animals to be boarded while they evacuated north to family, shelters or hotels that weren't pet-friendly.

"I'm really busy," was the first thing Cara said.

"I'm sorry. But there's something I need to talk to you about. Someone placed a game camera at the gate to our property," I blurted, even though it wasn't the best time.

"What? When did this happen?" she asked, her eyes growing dark. I realized she was thinking that this was more news I'd kept from her.

"I just found the camera this morning. I took it in and let Shantel process it."

"This is crazy." She was clearly having a hard time with this new information combined with everything else she was dealing with at the moment. I felt like crap for throwing it on her, but what choice did I have?

"You won't get any argument from me."

"Do you have any idea who put the camera there?"

"Blake Klein? Maybe the man whose body we found last night?"

"Why him?"

"We found Klein's business card in his pocket, so maybe he was working for him," I said as Cara glanced over at the counter where a man with an overexcited Boxer was trying to fill out paperwork. Gayle, the receptionist, was trying to help him while simultaneously taking a credit card from a man with a cat in a carrier. She glanced at Cara with a frantic expression on her face.

"Look, I know you need to go back to work. I only came here because I needed to tell you about this and to let you know that I'll go home and take care of Alvin and Ivy. I don't want you at the house alone until we get this figured out."

Cara was silent for a moment and I knew she wanted to tell me that she could take care of herself. But with everything else going on, she let it go. "Okay," she said, then began to rattle off a list of things I needed to pack for the animals.

"I already did most of that this morning," I said.

She took my hand. "You be careful."

When I got back to the office, it was unnervingly quiet and dark. Charley had finished boarding all the windows and almost everyone had left for their storm assignments.

Pete was still at his desk and there was a large cooler on mine.

"What's this?" I asked. After a couple years of working violent crimes, I was wary of packages left on my desk. My vivid imagination was already envisioning the cooler packed with human remains.

"When I told Sarah you were going to be here by yourself, she insisted on sending you a care package. I swear she's the worst at buying out the store when there's a storm coming. There are at least ten cases of water at the house."

Having been assured there weren't any severed body parts in the cooler, I opened it and found it neatly packed with sandwiches, fruits and snacks to last me a week.

"I'll share with Charley."

"If Sarah had known Charley was going to be here too, I'd have been hefting around two coolers."

"You realize that when the power goes out and your neighbors see your lights on, they'll want to bring all their frozen food over to your place."

"And lounge around in our air conditioning. Yep. I've already got the 'no trespassing' signs ready to go up," he said, still thrilled at the idea of getting to use his generator.

"Is it big enough to run your air conditioner?"

"No. That was a bit of an exaggeration. It's not as big as your dad's."

"Let's hope he still has a job to pay for all that propane come November."

"Hey, maybe the storm will knock down the billboards and blow away all the yard signs," Pete suggested.

"That would be a silver lining. Hey, thanks for giving us that report from Baggie."

"Any time I can pawn one of my cases off on you, I'm glad to do it."

I told him what we'd learned from Baggie and I also told him about the game camera. I had a faint hope that the camera might be unrelated to the reemergence of Blake Klein. Pete knew everyone and everything in Adams County. Maybe he knew of some hunter who was putting homemade game cams on people's property with plans to go poaching.

"That's freaky," Pete said, his tone not at all reassuring. "You could put out your own camera and try to catch him when he comes to check on his camera."

"That's very *Spy vs. Spy*," I said. "Anyway, I probably botched that opportunity by removing the camera. If he sees it's gone, he's not going to hang around. He might even look for another camera knowing that I might try to catch him."

"Now you're getting in deep. Of course, if you're right and your victim placed the camera on your property, then he won't be coming out of the morgue to upload pictures."

"True that. None of it makes much sense."

"That's how most cases work. Until you understand the perpetrator's motive, it's difficult to make sense of the crime."

"Just seems like there's more smoke and mirrors than usual. And this storm is frustrating the hell out of me. I want to be out questioning people, not cooped up in here playing nursemaid to the office. If I knew who the guy was, then I could at least be doing background on him. But with no fingerprints and no DNA results for at least a month, there's not much I can do until I can get back out on the streets."

"You kids and your DNA." Pete was only ten years older than me, but sometimes he enjoyed playing the crusty old lawman. "Back in my day, we'd spend hours going over mugshots if we needed to identify a suspect who might have a criminal record. Hey, whaddayaknow, you're going to *have* hours to look at mugshots. What luck!"

"Actually, that's a good idea. By the way, take another look at him." I pulled the victim's picture up on my phone. "Are you sure you don't recognize him?"

Pete looked long and hard. "No. He's definitely not from Adams County. I don't even see any family resemblance to anyone who is." Like I said, Pete knew everybody.

Pete headed out to his assignment at the elementary school and I looked at my watch. I had a little time before I needed to start checking in with the emergency management team. I downloaded the victim's picture to my computer so I could have his image on the screen side by side with the mugshots. How many mugshots could there be of white males thirty to forty years old? Five thousand, ten, twenty? The hurricane probably wouldn't last long enough for me to find him. But it was just like the lottery. I could find him in the first hundred records I looked at. Like my mother used to say, it was better to have luck than skill any day.

I logged into the National Crime Information Center database and plugged in my search criteria, being generous with both the age range and the location. I started with the southeastern United States.

As I scrolled and scrolled, I began to sympathize with all the witnesses I had made look through mugshots. Even with the victim's picture right in front of me, after looking at forty or fifty mugshots, I had to consciously look back at the picture and remind myself who I was looking for.

Luke finally arrived after I'd been at it for almost an hour. Who would have thought there were so many bad guys?

"I got two more like this," he said, dropping a Smirnoff's box full of notes and papers on Klein onto my desk.

I helped him bring in the rest of the files. The oak trees in the parking lot were swaying back and forth as gusts of wind whipped through them.

"Beginning to get wild out here," Luke said.

Since I had the building to myself, we took the boxes into our large conference room and spread everything out on the table.

"Any luck figuring out who the dead guy is?" Luke asked.

"How good are you with faces?"

"Pretty good, I guess," he said, falling into my trap.

"Have I got a job for you!"

I brought my laptop into the conference room so Luke could take over my search while I went through his files. I wanted him close at hand so that, if I had any questions, I didn't have to hunt for him.

"Wowee! Who would have thought there are so many guys who fit the description?"

"And those are just the ones that were arrested in the southeast," I said, and saw his usual good humor fade from his face as he calculated how long the search might take. "I've already looked at seven hundred of them."

"Guess I couldn't get a margarita."

"That would be a big old no."

"This is the lamest hurricane party I've ever been to," Luke said as he settled down to the job.

I looked at the table full of paper and wondered where to start. I spent time laying everything out chronologically, based on when events had happened, not when the reports had been written.

"The man was always a sleaze," I said after a while.

"That's the takeaway. He grew up poor and hated it. Talking to people from his childhood, they told me how he just wanted to make money. Period. Tried a dozen different schemes before he was even out of high school. Was a good salesman. A couple of times he did all right, but that wasn't good enough for him. A classmate of his said that he'd always be mad, whatever the result. He'd make a hundred dollars selling a set of golf clubs and he'd be angry that he didn't make two hundred. He bought a car once, cleaned it up, flipped it for a thousand and then spent the next month pissed that he hadn't made two thousand. That's a recipe for one unhappy life." Luke didn't look up as he talked; he just stared at the screen and clicked the mouse.

"I can sort of see all the parts coming together. He sold electronics for a couple years before going into a security business with a partner. What a joke. But he must have learned a lot about installing cameras."

"And as you read through, you'll see that he got more and more upset that he wasn't making the kind of money he wanted. Should have been a clue to everyone when he was suddenly a happier guy."

"You've done a thorough job in a short amount of time. It's only been a couple months."

"I like research. Plus I'd already been following him for a couple years. I've got enough background on him for a book. I just need to figure out what the story is going to be."

"And the ending could turn out to be a bit different than you thought."

"I gotta say, it crossed my mind that this could be a whole new chapter. And if he is still alive and doing bad shit, then that could raise his profile. Maybe even make him interesting enough for me to get a *real* book deal."

"Let's hope he doesn't become that interesting."

"The guy was, or is, a real psychopath. He could do the

whole Ted Bundy thing of turning on the charm when he wanted to, and then, with a flip of the switch, go into monster mode."

"Your Bundy analogy could be pretty apt. 'Cause if he's behind these latest deaths, he's getting more and more unhinged. There doesn't seem to be a money angle to it."

"Unless he was taking a cut from the guy who was robbing the drug dealers."

"That would be small potatoes for him. Of course, we haven't found the money or the drugs. We haven't even figured out where the dead guy was living, so everything is still on the table."

"Do you think he went into a partnership with your victim?"

"Or maybe they didn't even meet until Klein killed him."

"Hadn't thought of that. He kills him and puts his card in his wallet as a kind of signature."

"Like I said, everything is on the table."

"Hey!" Luke exclaimed and I looked up.

"What?"

"Hey, hey, I got a maybe here," he said excitedly. I got up to look, though it seemed unlikely he could have stumbled upon our victim that fast.

"Man, if it's not him then it's his twin brother."

I looked over his shoulder. He'd lined the picture of the victim up next to the mugshot of a man named Stevie Ray Hutton. I had to admit there was a strong resemblance. I looked at the chin and the ears. Ears in particular are facial landmarks that are hard to change unless you get into lobe stretching or other body modification. Luckily, that didn't seem to be the case with either the victim or the guy in the mugshot.

"I've got a couple more angles on my phone," I said, pulling them up. A person can look very different depending on the perspective. I'd picked out people from a mugshot, but as soon as I saw them in real life, I realized they didn't look anything like the person I was searching for. That's one of the reasons they take pictures from different angles when booking criminals into jail.

I held my phone next to the mugshot.

"I got to agree with you. These are dead ringers. And just for the record, they're both assholes so I don't feel bad about the pun. Let me see if I can pull up Stevie's full criminal history and figure out where he is now."

"With luck, he's in your morgue," Luke said.

"Talk about luck. You only looked at three or four percent of the mugshots and came up with a match. You've used up your lottery win."

"If it's him then it'll be worth the loss of my lotto millions."

CHAPTER TWELVE

I sat down beside Luke and pulled the laptop in front of me to get a better look at Hutton's record.

"Not a good guy. Drugs, assault, carjacking. Last arrested four years ago for assault in Liberty County. Convicted and received two years. Released early on probation. To give you an idea how well that worked, he's currently wanted for probation violation."

I pulled out my phone and contacted the Florida Department of Corrections. Five minutes later I had the number of his probation officer. I crossed my fingers that the man wasn't too busy with storm prep to take my call. Luck was with me.

After providing my bona fides, I said, "I'm looking for information on Stevie Ray Hutton. I believe you're his probation officer?"

"Hold on," the man said, and I heard the clicking of a keyboard in the background. "I *was*. He came in for two visits and then disappeared, so he's officially off my roles. I'm looking at his picture now. Yeah, I remember this guy. He gave me the creeps. There are men and women you think have got a good shot at making a decent life once they get out of prison. He wasn't one of them. Stevie fell solidly into the hug-your-child-close-to-you category."

"I think he's turned up dead here," I said.

"Let me be the first to say: good."

"Unfortunately, he'd already done enough bad stuff to make us all happy he won't be walking the streets anymore."

"Killed?"

"Yes."

"Sorry. Now you have to pretend to care and look for his killer."

"Exactly. But before we get too far ahead of ourselves, we have a problem with identifying his body. He managed to scrape and burn his fingerprints off."

"That probably made a lot of sense considering his career path. Not to worry, though, we should have his DNA on file."

"That's good, but it's going to take a while to get our body's DNA processed. You only saw him a couple of times, but is there anything you can remember that stood out and might help identify him? I didn't see any notes in his record about identifiable scars."

"Those arrest records aren't always the most complete. I can pull up his prison record. That will have the best physical description. We might even have dental records." There was more clicking, then he said, "You're in luck. He had a couple busted teeth while in jail and got some dental work done. You know, *I* don't get free dental care. Anyway, I can email you copies of his dental records."

"Perfect."

"Let me know if it's him. I'll do the work to get him entered into our system as deceased and start the paperwork to have his warrants rescinded." I gave him my email and, before we'd said our goodbyes, the information was in my inbox.

"An efficient bureaucrat," Luke observed.

"They make them."

I dialed Dr. Darzi's office. "Don't you know there's a hurricane bearing down on us?" he said in mock panic.

"And yet you're still in your office."

"I see my young interns getting all worked up. What should we buy? Are we closing early? Will the office be open tomorrow? What do they think, that the world stops for a little wind and rain?"

"Then you won't mind comparing some dental records with the body that Linda and Ann picked up last night?"

"Those two. They will be the death of me. Yes, dental records are good. I always feel better when we can put a proper name on the forms. Send them over and I'll personally check them and get back to you within the hour."

He was good as his word. "I am typing the name 'Stevie Ray Hutton' as we speak," Darzi told me when I answered my phone.

I barely had a chance to thank him before Darlene called to check in with me.

"Aren't you playing footsie with your boyfriend?" I asked her.

"It's actually pretty crazy over here. I've already broken up one domestic dispute between a husband and wife. She was wigging out that he hadn't packed her phone charger. So what did she do? She threw her phone at him and smashed it. It was a freaking iPhone. There are probably two dozen people here who could have lent her a charger. I've already decided: when the apocalypse comes, I'm not workin' it!"

"Did you call me just to tell me how much fun you're having?"

"No, I called 'cause I know where our victim was living." I swear I could actually see her smug smile through the phone.

"That's nice, but I already know his real name," I said with what I hoped was an equally smug expression on my face.

"Bullshit," she shot back.

"Stevie Ray Hutton."

"You made that up. That's the name of a serial killer."

"I didn't make it up and I admit I had the same thought

when I saw his name. Okay, I shared. Your turn."

"He's staying at a campground just off the interstate one exit east."

"How'd you pull that out of your hat?"

"First, he didn't seem to have any ties to the county, so he must have been holed up somewhere. Second, I assumed he wouldn't want to stay in some dive in Adams County; there'd be too much risk of running into someone he just stuck up. I struck out with hotels in Tallahassee. It was actually Hondo who suggested the campground. It's kind of seedy. He said he's been out there on a couple of calls. The fees are cheap and people leave you alone."

I looked at my watch, then took a quick glance at the latest weather satellite map on my laptop. "We're agreed that he was dumped at the Ditch, so where he was staying could be a crime scene. I'm going to head over there and check it out before the storm gets much worse."

"Not without me, buster. This is my lead."

"Fine, I'll pick you up. The high school is on the way to the interstate."

"Grab a bunch of evidence bags and another fingerprint kit. The woman I talked to at the campground said he was living in a tent. With the storm coming in, we may need to just bag everything rather than take a chance of it getting blown or washed away."

"Agreed. I'm on my way." I was up and headed for the door before I disconnected the call.

"What do you want me to do?" Luke asked, sounding a little lost.

"Stay here and try to find a connection between Hutton, Ruddy Lynch and Blake Klein. Anything that seems to provide a tie between any of them. Check out their histories. Were they ever in the same town or school or business at the same time?"

"Got it."

I ran into Charley Wright out in the hall.

"Hey, Larry, I had a couple cots sent over for us," he

said.

"Thanks, Charley. I'm going to run out, but when I get back I'll be here for the duration."

"Not a problem," he said good-naturedly, then pointed to Luke in the conference room. "Is he staying too? I can get an extra cot."

"He probably is, but the two cots will be enough. I doubt we'll all be napping at the same time."

The parking lot of the high school looked like Walmart on Black Friday, only with more RVs, trailers and boats. Darlene was waiting for me under the awning that led to the gym. She hopped into my car almost before I could park it.

"Crazy people," she muttered.

"You can probably take off your badge," I told her. She was wearing a tag that identified her as part of the emergency management team.

"Didn't do much good anyway. Nobody paid any attention to me." She took it off and tossed it on the seat. "But don't let me go back in there without it. I'm just glad I'm not with the highway patrol. Sounds like there are still a whole bunch of folks on the road. It would help if they didn't insist on trying to haul all their boats and campers with them."

"People want to save what they can. What is the current projection?"

"Still landing west of us as a Category 3."

"Good job finding Hutton's hideout."

"I'm glad I found it before this storm got to it. If he really was living in a tent, then there probably won't be much left of it after tomorrow."

"We've been racing against time with this one."

I took the entrance ramp and realized there was no point trying to merge with the traffic going east. Thankful for the blue lights in the grill of my unmarked, I turned them on and drove down the breakdown lane. The traffic on I-10 was moving about ten miles an hour. I could go thirty on the shoulder.

"This state has gotten lucky for years. One day that luck'll run out and a bunch of folks are gonna get caught out on the road when a real monster hurricane hits," Darlene said.

"Aren't you a ray of sunshine peeking through the clouds," I kidded her. I didn't think I'd ever seen Darlene that gloomy. "You really don't like storms."

"The storm is only part of what bothers me. There's just something about watching people flee that gets to me."

"Maybe you're reincarnated and whoever you were in your past life had to run before an invading army," I said lightly.

"You joke, but that's what it feels like. Some sort of traumatic event that I can't quite remember," she answered, her voice deadly serious.

You never know what haunts other people, I thought. Aloud, I said, "You're creeping me out. Where exactly is this campground?"

"Next exit. It's called Campers Haven and is about a mile off the interstate."

"I see the sign," I said, eager to escape the highway. Even with the flashing blue lights, we were getting glared at by passengers in other cars.

A long line of cars, trucks and campers announced the entrance to the campground. There must have been thirty vehicles lined up at the office. I pulled around them and parked behind the building.

"I can give you a place to park, but you aren't going to have electric," a woman was saying as we walked inside. The man in front of her looked angry and tired in equal measures. He squinted and licked his lips, looking like he was considering jumping the counter.

"How much for the square of dirt to park on?" he barked.

"Fifty dollars a night." The woman didn't miss a beat.

"Whatever," he said, thrusting his hand in his pocket and yanking out his wallet.

When the woman turned to get a registration form for the man to fill out, Darlene took the opportunity to talk with her.

"I'm Deputy Darlene Marks. I think I spoke to you earlier." She held up her badge and the woman glanced at it.

"We had to move his tent," she said.

"I told you we wanted it preserved," Darlene said, gritting her teeth.

"Do you see this?" The woman waved at all the vehicles outside and the half dozen people waiting in the office. "What do you expect us to do? He hadn't paid in a couple days. I tried to call the number he left."

"I told you he was dead." Darlene enunciated each word as though she was speaking to an idiot.

"Which is probably why he didn't answer," the woman admitted. "Look, we just took the stakes out and pulled it out of the way. We didn't mess with anything inside. Are you all going to pay what he owed us for those two nights?"

I saw the color rise in Darlene's cheeks and grabbed her arm, stopping her from saying whatever was bubbling up from her darker nature. I was sure that every person in the office had a phone and wouldn't hesitate to use it. I didn't want to see Darlene go viral on YouTube.

"Just show us where the tent is," I told the woman. She looked at me like she wanted to say something, but instead she turned her head and screamed for someone named Simon.

"Show these two where we put that tent we moved," she told a round young man who appeared out of a back room. The boy, who looked to be around fifteen, stared at us and nodded.

We followed the kid through a maze of parked cars, RVs and tents. Next to the public bathrooms, a half-folded tent was leaning against the block wall.

"That's it," he said and left without another word.

"Lovely place for a holiday," Darlene grumbled.

"At least it's not raining right this minute," I said. Right on cue came several rumbles of thunder.

We put on protective suits and gloves, and bags over our shoes.

"Let's look through everything, bag up anything we think is important, then roll up the rest in the tent and take the whole thing back to Shantel," I said.

"Sounds like a plan."

Darlene unzipped the tent and crawled inside. I got down on my knees in the mud and stuck my head through the opening. There was a sleeping bag and a medium-size duffel bag, and the odor in the tent was vintage locker room. A pair of socks and some underwear were inside the sleeping bag.

"I can't say I think much of his personal hygiene," I said as Darlene unzipped the duffel bag.

"This is more like it," she said, shining a small flashlight inside the bag.

"What?"

"There are spent shell casings and some live ammo in the bottom of the bag. Nine millimeter from the look of... Wait, there are some forty-fives here too." She reached inside the bag. "There's a 1911 wrapped up in a T-shirt. Some drug bags. All of them look empty except for some white residue. No phone. No laptop or tablet. A piece of paper. Crap!"

"What?" I had an urge to try crawling in after her, but I knew how silly it would be and restrained myself.

"There's an address on the paper." She paused, apparently for dramatic effect. "It's the sheriff's office."

"What the hell... That doesn't make much sense."

"Hold your stockings up. Here's some more paper with half a dozen addresses. They all look like they're in Adams County. One of them is Hitdawg's house."

"Someone gave him a list of houses to hit?"

"I'd say that's a good working theory. I could dig through this for a while, but it'd be best to take it back to the office where Shantel can process it. The more I rummage, the more likely I am to damage or compromise evidence. Plus, I can't breathe in here."

I left her to guard the tent while I went to get the car. It took me almost half an hour to get back because I had to convince a middle-aged couple with a herd of Chihuahuas that they were blocking me in with their enormous RV. Another band of wind and rain hit just as we wrestled the tent into the back seat.

I dropped a wet and reluctant Darlene off at the high school. She wanted to go back to the office with me and pick through our loot from the campground. I don't think she was looking forward to wading back into the jumble of refugees.

"Hondo will be here with you," I said cheerfully.

"You're picking up a lot of sass hanging around me," she said and got out.

I headed for home, thinking I'd almost waited too late to take Alvin and Ivy to Dad's. I could feel the wind pushing the car as I drove. The gusts had to be almost forty-five miles an hour now. I pulled up to my gate and sat in the car for a minute, looking around. Better to be safe than sorry, but nothing seemed unusual or out of place. Of course, with the wind and rain, someone could have been standing a hundred feet away and I wouldn't have been able to see them.

I was soaked by the time I got to my small porch. The normally docile live oaks in my front yard were excitedly waving their branches in the wind.

Inside, I taped up all the windows, emptied the icemaker and turned it off, along with almost everything else that ran on electricity. I coaxed and cajoled Alvin into a trip outside, holding onto his leash while he dived under the porch to pee on one of the support posts before dashing back inside. Then came the tricky part.

We'd set up their travel crates on the bed in the guestroom. I carefully picked up the suspicious Ivy, but as soon as I got near the doorway, she started to struggle. Even with the crate standing on end with the door already open, it was like trying to cram an octopus with claws into a plastic bag.

Alvin was easy by comparison. A few kind words and some treats and I was able to ease him into his crate.

Before leaving the house, I called Cara to make sure she hadn't thought of something I hadn't.

"We're almost done here. Scott has volunteered to stay at the clinic with the animals," Cara said, referring to one of the clinic's young kennel techs.

"There's a generator, right?"

"Yep, and Dr. Barnhill made Scott start it up to prove he knew how to use it. And also to make sure it worked. I'm heading over to the emergency management center now."

"I'll text you after I get the animals safely delivered to Dad's."

As we said goodbye, I could still feel the distance that had been created by our argument about Klein's hidden cameras. It caused me to spend another ten minutes walking through the house, looking for hidden cameras or microphones. *Rein in the paranoia, Larry*, I told myself. Finally convinced there was nothing more I could do at the house, I loaded the car and drove off to the sounds of angry cat.

When I got to Dad's, I almost laughed when I saw Finn and Mac standing in their paddock. Dad had painted their names, his phone number and address on both of them. It looked like they were hanging their heads in embarrassment, though they were probably just tired of all the wind and rain.

I went inside to make sure the beast was restrained before I tried to bring a very pissed-off Ivy and a confused Alvin into the mix. Mauser was having the time of his life with so many of his fans under one roof. He went zooming from me to Jamie, his sitter, then on to Genie, Dad's girlfriend, and from her to her son, Jimmy, who was laughing hysterically at Mauser's antics.

"I've got him," Jamie said, putting a harness on Mauser.

Once I'd settled Ivy in a bedroom with her litter pan, water, food and a secure door between her and Mauser, I brought Alvin in and let him and Mauser get reacquainted.

Within a few minutes the hierarchy was established, with Alvin clearly the alpha dog.

"You all settled in for the duration?" I asked Genie.

"I think so. Jimmy isn't happy he's missing work," she said, looking over at her son who was meeting Alvin for the first time.

Jimmy was close to my age and had Down Syndrome. Genie used to babysit me, and Jimmy and I had often played together. After Genie's husband left her, she'd moved to Tallahassee with Jimmy, where she was now the manager of an upscale restaurant. When Dad had met her again after many years, I think their shared memories of our younger years had bridged a gap of sorrow for both of them.

"I hate missing work," Jimmy said as he stroked Alvin, who was enjoying being the center of attention, to Mauser's intense irritation. The Dane retaliated by trying to sit on Jimmy.

"This will be over soon," I told him.

"Just a bunch of wind and rain," he said dismissively, laughing as he pushed Mauser off of him. "I do like being at Uncle Ted's, though."

Genie and Jamie assured me they would make sure that Ivy also got some attention, then I headed back out into the storm.

CHAPTER THIRTEEN

The sun was going down as I parked at the office, but it was hard to tell with the dark clouds racing across the sky. There was no doubt that we were on the edge of a hurricane now as street signs rocked under the heavy wind gusts. The streets were almost empty as most people had already found places to hunker down and wait out the storm. Only the gas stations were still open, though most of the pumps were bagged.

I assumed the front door was locked and went around to the back of the office, using my passkey to get in.

"It's starting to blow out there," Charley said, meeting me at the door and holding it for me as I carried in several bags of evidence from Hutton's tent.

I took everything down to Shantel's empty lair and put the bags on the table, staring at them for a moment. What I should have done was put everything in a locker until Shantel could go through it all after the storm. And if it hadn't been for the fact that the case might have something to do with the camera on my property, then I would have gladly left it all for later. But what if there was a piece of evidence in those bags that was actionable? Something I could pursue right then.

I pulled on gloves and set up a video camera so I could record everything I did with the evidence. I didn't want some defense attorney claiming I'd mishandled anything. Once everything was set up, I tackled the duffel bag first. I took everything out and set it on the table. My plan was to examine each object and then bag them individually.

Just emptying the bag took a while. There were half a dozen spent rounds and a dozen loose cartridges in the bottom of the bag. There was also a phone charger, but no phone. At least it told us he'd had a Samsung model at one time. That was the trouble with modern electronic devices. It was often all or nothing. Time was, a bad guy could be expected to leave magazines, books, notes, pictures and maybe even an address book behind, but now people could keep all of that on their phones. If you found their phone, you were golden. But right now we had zilch.

I unwrapped the 1911 very carefully. It was a Remington and in pretty good shape. Someone had made an attempt to file off the serial number, giving me a good idea that it was stolen. I removed the magazine and bagged it before checking the chamber. There was a round inside, so I pulled the slide back and let the round drop softly into its own evidence bag.

When I was done with the handgun, a thought occurred to me. I pulled out my phone and dialed Darlene.

"What's up, Sam Spade?"

"Be nice. I'm being thoughtful," I said.

"Do tell."

"You've used FaceTime, right?"

"Yep, Hondo and I do it all the time."

"I don't want to hear about it!" I shouted to stop her from going any further with that thought. "My point is, I'm going through Hutton's stuff and thought you could join me via FaceTime."

"I knew you couldn't resist. Let's do this."

It took me a minute to get everything set up so she could watch, then I showed her what I'd done so far.

"I wonder if he used that .45 for his hold-ups. Nothing like a big steel 1911 to intimidate your victims."

"Maybe, though Baggie said his gun was black."

"Could look black in the dark."

"Agreed. But we know he probably had a nine millimeter to go with the casings and cartridges we found."

Next I pulled out some clothes. Nothing interesting, just generic T-shirts and jeans.

"He was a little light on underwear," Darlene said with a tinge of disgust in her voice.

"Now this is interesting," I said, holding up two pill bottles that were both almost empty. The prescription labels were in his real name and were from the Florida Department of Corrections. I showed her the bottles.

"Those are anti-psychotics. That's a shocker. Why do I think he hasn't been taking them recently?"

"We need to let Darzi know so he can request that the toxicology screening look for traces of them in Hutton's system. I'm with you in thinking there won't be much."

"If he stopped taking them abruptly, then that could explain his extreme self-destructive behavior recently," Darlene pointed out.

"You could certainly classify holding up drug dealers and addicts as self-destructive."

We didn't find much else in the bag. The sleeping bag yielded only the socks and underwear, which I bagged like they were toxic waste.

"Thanks, Darlene. I guess I'll ask Charley to help me bring in the tent."

We hauled the tent into the evidence room and bagged it as best we could. It seemed like pretty rash handling of evidence, but I didn't have many options.

When we were finished, I looked at my watch. I'd spent over an hour sorting and stashing the evidence from Hutton's campsite. I hadn't even thought to check in with Luke yet.

He'll be excited to hear what we found, I thought as I walked to the conference room.

I was a little creeped out by how quiet the building was. Even at night and on weekends there was some sort of activity at the office. Deputies on patrol frequently used it as a pit stop for writing reports, changing clothes, working out or catching a snack.

The conference room door was open just a crack, which struck me as odd. I'd have sworn it was wide open when I'd left Luke there earlier. *Maybe Charley was making some noise and Luke closed the door for privacy*, I thought. Even still, I pushed the door open with my shoulder instead of using the doorknob.

I was used to seeing the unexpected when I was on duty, but what I saw when I entered the room shocked me as much as it would have in my own home. Luke was lying on his stomach on the floor. The back of his head and much of his shirt was covered with blood. For a moment I froze, not because I was scared but because my rational mind was telling me to stop and think. I wanted to rush over to him, but if he was already dead it wouldn't do any good and, in fact, could harm the crime scene. My eyes took in the room and then refocused on Luke. Even with all the blood, there was something about the color of his skin that told me he was alive.

I hurried over to him and bent down, placing two fingers against his neck. Sure enough, there was a slow, weak bump against my fingers. I called 911, but even after I identified myself, I was told that ambulance service was on a priority basis and could be stopped at any moment due to high winds. Pissed off, I hung up rather than argue with the dispatcher. Then I remembered that Dr. Patrick should be right across the street at the emergency management center. I called Dad.

"Dr. Patrick's here. We'll be there in five," he said and hung up.

I was glad they were coming, but Luke had suffered severe head trauma. A doctor wasn't going to be enough. I didn't need a medical degree to know that he needed a hospital. I grabbed my phone again and called Darlene. After a quick explanation, she handed me over to Hondo.

"He needs to be transported," the EMT said after I told him what had happened.

"Dispatch said you all might be shut down."

"Nobody gonna shut me down. You'd be surprised how often my radio doesn't work. I'm on the way."

Dad and Dr. Patrick arrived as soon as I hung up with Hondo.

"Ambulance is on the way," I said.

"They're still running?" Dr. Patrick said, sounding surprised. "Good. He needs to get to the hospital as soon as possible." I helped him turn Luke over and he made sure his airways were clear. "Get a blanket," Dr. Patrick instructed me.

I ran back to the maintenance room where Charley had set up a bed for himself.

"What's going on?" he asked, surprised when I burst into the room and grabbed the blanket off the cot.

"Luke's been attacked in the conference room."

"Is he hurt bad?" Charley asked as he followed me back to the conference room.

"The front door was unlocked," Dad said, his face set in a frustrated glower. Someone was going to be raked over the coals for that.

"The security cameras should give us an idea who did this," I said and automatically looked up to the camera in the corner of the conference room. "Shit!" I said involuntarily. The lens of the camera had been covered in spray paint.

Dad followed my eyes. His expression went from glower to fury in a moment.

"I've got something to tell you," I said, but before I could say more, Darlene, Hondo and an EMT I didn't know came through the door.

"We've got a stretcher, Doc," Hondo said.

Dr. Patrick looked at him. I thought I saw frustration on

his face. I imagined it was a common emotion for conscientious doctors. How often are all of their skills and knowledge shown to be futile in the face of our fragile bodies?

"He's as stable as he can be," Dr. Patrick said, standing up. Hondo and the other man set the stretcher next to Luke and, gently and efficiently, they loaded him up and rolled him out of the room. Darlene and Dr. Patrick followed them.

"I'll call the ER and tell them what to expect," he said.

"Let's clear the building," Dad said. "You take the back, I'll take the front and we'll meet at my office."

It took us twenty minutes to do a thorough sweep of the building. Every door, every office, every bathroom, every closet and window was checked. Before I headed to Dad's office, I told Charley it was okay for him to return to the maintenance room and that I'd talk with him later. It was possible he might have heard something when Luke was attacked, but I wanted to check the other camera footage with Dad first.

Dad was still holding his engraved Glock 21 when I entered his office. He'd carried a Colt 1911 most of his career until recently. He'd told me that the idea of facing an active shooter situation with only eight rounds in the gun was too much of a handicap. I noticed he was even using extended magazines.

He re-holstered the gun and turned to me. "We can access the rest of the cameras from here."

When he brought up the images on his computer, we found the intruder easily. All we had to do was rewind to the point just before the image from a particular camera went dark. The first one was at the entrance. A dark figure in a hoodie came up to the camera. The person was wearing gloves and, when he got close to the camera, he looked up. Under the hood, he wore a ski mask and glasses that made it impossible to see any facial features. As soon as he looked up, he raised his right hand. For a second, there was the image of a spray can and then the video went dark.

We followed his trail through the building as he blacked out each camera. When we came to the conference room video, we saw Luke's back hunched over his laptop. This time the figure crept in and struck Luke with a foot-long pipe before turning and painting over the camera.

When the video was finished, I filled Dad in on everything I knew about Stevie Ray Hutton, the camera I'd found at my property and the possibility of a connection to Blake Klein.

"Klein. Hell! I want this guy," he said, pointing at the images on the computer. "I don't care if it's really Klein or someone else. But no one comes into my office and attacks an innocent man."

"If it's Klein, then why hasn't he gone after me or you? Why all these oblique attacks?"

The words were hardly out of my mouth before a horrible thought occurred to me. With my heart rate jumping into triple digits, I pulled out my phone and called Cara, silently begging for her to pick up. But all I heard was ringing until her voicemail answered.

I turned to Dad. "Cara's not answering her phone."

"I saw her at the emergency management center about an hour ago. Let's go."

I yelled for Charley to lock the doors as we dove out into the wind and driving rain. I didn't know if the roar in my ears was the storm or the beat of my heart. Dad told me later that I didn't even look when I ran across the street.

At the jail, I pushed through the side doors that led directly into the emergency management center. There was so much noise and activity from the thirty or so people standing about or talking on their phones, not to mention the dispatchers working emergency calls, that no one seemed to notice when I came barging through the door.

"Hey!" I shouted. A few people turned and looked at me, but I still didn't have the attention of even half the room. For one insane moment I thought about taking my gun out and firing it in the air, but then I heard an ear-piercing shriek from behind me. I turned to see Dad with a chrome whistle in his mouth.

"Always carry a whistle," he said.

I turned back to see a sea of shocked faces. "Has anyone seen Cara Laursen?"

"I saw her maybe an hour ago," said Freddy Kimble from public works.

"Last time I saw her, she was talking on her phone," Ray Alverez, a supervisor with the electric company, tossed out.

"Has anyone seen her in the last half hour?" I asked.

"What's she look like? I don't think I know her," said an older woman from the county's water department.

"Red hair, about this tall," I said, holding my hand out level with my shoulders. Then I pulled up the best picture of Cara that I could find on my phone and handed it to the woman. Several other people came up and looked over her shoulder until she passed it back to them. There was some comparing of notes before the consensus was reached that Cara hadn't been in the room for at least half an hour.

Dad stepped up. "Someone was assaulted across the street. We have reason to think that Cara could be in danger."

"Can you check the security cameras over here?" I asked Dad. "I'm going outside to look for her car."

"Radio me if you find anything," he said, and we each grabbed a radio from the bank of chargers by the door.

"I'll be glad to help in the search," Ray Alverez said. He was a handsome man with a slight Hispanic accent.

"Thanks! But let me check on her car first. Right now I don't want to take a chance of disturbing any evidence. If I don't find anything, we'll broaden the search."

Ray nodded. Several other people had stepped up to volunteer with him, but they stood back when they heard my answer. I pulled out my flashlight and headed back out into the storm.

There were a lot of vehicles in the parking lot. The jail

had called in two shifts' worth of staff to make sure they had enough manpower to cover a twenty-four or forty-eight-hour cycle during the storm. In addition to those of the deputies and civilians manning the jail, there were the cars and trucks of all the people manning the emergency management center. With the rain coming down so hard that the light from the streetlamps could barely cut through it, it was almost impossible to see more than ten feet in front of me. I finally found Cara's car after walking half the lot.

The car was locked. Using the flashlight, I tried to look through the windows but couldn't make out anything through the rain. I scanned the ground around the car, but there was nothing there.

I was soaked, miserable and scared to death that something had happened to Cara. There was a loud bang behind me and I flinched, then turned in time to see all the streetlights go out and sparks fly from a blown transformer.

"I found the car, but there's no sign of Cara," I told Dad over the radio.

"I'm coming out," he said, surprising me.

"What's going on?"

"Tell you when I get out there."

I met him at the main entrance to the jail and we huddled by the doors to get out of the worst of the rain. The look on his face was pure fury.

"There's no video from several of the outdoor cameras around the time Cara went missing," he said through clenched teeth.

He walked out into the rain to look up at the cameras. I followed him, but it was impossible to tell what was wrong with the cameras and we were forced to retreat back to the shelter of the building.

"With this storm, someone could have shot them with a .22 and no one would have heard it. McElroy was working the security desk and he just figured the storm had knocked them out. I want to kick his ass, but I can't blame him. With all the lightning and wind, the cameras could have easily been compromised. He was more focused on the images from inside the jail." Dad's frustration was close to boiling over and mine wasn't far behind. "There was footage of Cara arriving. Everything looked normal then, but the rain made it difficult to see much."

"What about inside the center?"

"There aren't any cameras inside. Prisoners aren't allowed over there, and the room is only used for meetings when there's no emergency. We didn't see the point in installing them."

"We have to find Cara," I said unnecessarily. I tried to figure out what the next move should be, but I was finding it hard to focus.

"We need to think. Those cameras mean something," Dad said.

"He probably didn't want us to see him approach the building. The cameras are mounted too high on the roof for him to try the same trick he used in the sheriff's office."

"Same person. Are we going with that?" Dad said, and I appreciated that he was deferring some of the decision to me.

"I can't see this as a coincidence, not after the attack on Luke. Cara wouldn't wander off in this storm without letting someone know. And I'd give even money that the email and the card left in Hutton's pocket are all part of it too. I don't know if that was Blake Klein on the video from next door or if he's got someone working with him, but I intend to nail whatever bastard is behind it to the wall. Come on. Let's get a search party to thoroughly check inside and outside the building."

"I suggest going out in small groups," Dad said. "I know that most evidence has probably already been washed away in the storm, but we don't want to take even a small risk that something important could be trampled or lost. We can use some of the deputies working the jail. With their double shift onsite, it won't leave them shorthanded."

"Thank you."

"Sustained winds are close to fifty miles an hour now. We're going to have to tell all first responders to end active efforts soon."

"I understand," I said, knowing Dad hadn't wanted to acknowledge the fact we wouldn't be able to send search parties out beyond the buildings if we didn't find Cara right away.

I followed him inside the jail where he headed straight back to the office of Captain Ross Bennett, who commanded the jail. Dad had already talked to Bennett when he reviewed the camera footage, so the captain didn't need much time to get up to speed.

We decided we'd go out in two groups of three, with Dad and I both leading a group. Captain Bennett drafted four deputies from the jail to help. I recognized two of them. Meghan Lawson had worked patrol until she'd suffered a bad knee injury in a car accident. Corporal Jerry Franks had been a great patrol officer, but his wife had badgered him to take a job at the jail where she felt he'd be safer and have more regular hours. The other two were younger deputies with less than a year on the job.

Dad took the younger deputies to search the inside of the building while Meghan and Jerry went with me to search the exterior and out-buildings.

We searched for half an hour and found nothing. I was headed back to the jail, walking up the side of the annex toward the main entrance of the emergency management center, when my flashlight illuminated something shiny on the ground. I knelt down to look and my breath turned shallow and rapid when I realized what I was seeing. It was the heart from the necklace I'd given Cara for her birthday.

CHAPTER FOURTEEN

I was barely able to stop myself from reaching down to grab the heart. In an ideal situation, I should have taken a photo of it, but there wasn't any point. I'd have just ended up with a water-logged phone and a crappy picture. Instead, I pulled gloves and an evidence bag out of my pocket. I picked up the small heart and placed it in the bag before looking around to see if there were any other signs of a struggle. Where was the chain?

I took note of the spot, which was only ten feet from the entrance to the center, then headed back to the reception area of the jail where we'd all agreed to meet after the search.

"I found this by the door of the annex," I said, showing the heart to Dad. I swear I heard him growl. The necklace had been a special gift he'd bought for my mother and he'd encouraged me to give it to Cara.

"If it wasn't for this damn storm, we'd be able to get Leon County to send over their helicopter and use their FLIR camera. We've got a couple of handhelds, but they aren't going to do any good in this rain. Even a light rain interferes with them." Dad was talking to himself as much as me.

"I want to look at the security footage," I said.

"Okay. I'm going to talk to everyone in the center and see if we can start establishing a timeline. And don't forget about Charley. He still needs to be questioned."

"I know. I didn't think about him as a suspect since the camera over there showed someone entering the building from the outside. But... who knows at this point." My fear and frustration was making it hard to think. I had to keep pushing down the panicked voice that insisted I run around looking for Cara and remind myself that a methodical approach was the best way to get her back safely.

Captain Bennett took me into his office and showed me the footage from outside the annex.

"The sheriff said that's Cara," he said, pointing to an image on the screen made fuzzy by the rain.

It was definitely Cara. In the video, she ran through the rain up to the door of the center and opened it before stepping in and disappearing from the screen. About half an hour later, that camera and several others went blank in succession.

"I see why Dad thought someone might have shot them."

"Maybe with a .22. A BB gun wouldn't have done it. Of course, with this storm you could fire off a hunting rifle and no one would notice," Captain Bennett said.

"I want to see footage from any other cameras that face toward the front or rear entrance of the parking lot."

Bennett pulled up video from three different cameras. "These weren't damaged."

I ran them from fifteen minutes before the damage to the other cameras had occurred until the point we started searching for Cara.

"I can just see to the left of the entrance," I said, pointing to the image on the far side of the screen.

"You'd be able to see the road pretty well if it wasn't storming. In fact, you can see the sheriff's office across the street during the day and the lights from the building at night."

"I can see the occasional lights of cars passing by. So making two assumptions—that the person who abducted Cara would have had their car lights on and that they turned left—I don't see any car leaving the lot and going that direction."

"You can see a similar image on the right. But you can't see if the cars going by came out of the lot. The camera is shifted too far to the right for that."

"But by comparing car headlights that go from the left camera to the right with the timestamp, I can see if the ones on the right originated between the two."

"That makes sense."

We looked at the footage closely.

"No one drove out the front from the time that Cara was taken to the point that Dad and I showed up."

Captain Bennett pulled up the footage for the back parking lot. While the cameras in the back hadn't been damaged, most of them pointed at or near the building. Only one camera showed the exit to the back parking lot. Even with the rain and the occasional swaying branch obscuring the camera, it was clear that no vehicles had left the parking lot during the time of Cara's disappearance.

"They're still here," I said.

"Or they took her off property on foot. There are several neighborhoods within a block and the courthouse square isn't that far. As a matter of fact—"

I stopped him, not wanting a huge dose of reality now that I had some cause for hope. "I get it. There are other ways out. You'll save all this footage?"

I got a look that clearly asked what sort of idiot I thought he was. I thanked him for his help and escaped back to the emergency management center. Dad came over to me as soon as I was through the door.

"I called the FBI. They've assigned someone to the case and offered to do what they can over the phone until the storm passes. Once it's over, they'll be here within two hours to start the hunt for her."

"Good. But I've got an idea. I think someone here did this."

"Took her?"

"Yes." I told him about the evidence from the video cameras.

"So she could still be here," Dad said, and put in another call to Captain Bennett. "We're going to need those deputies again. And I want everyone in the building who has a car in the parking lot to hand over their keys with a note as to which car is theirs and roughly where it's parked. We need to check the trunk of every car. If they don't have a car with a trunk or a truck with a topper, then they don't have to hand over their keys. If they don't want us to search their vehicle, then they can come out in the storm and open it up for us. We're going to do the same with the folks over here in the center."

"We'll need to mark the cars as we search them," I said when he'd hung up.

"Tricky with this rain and wind. I guess we can tie crime scene tape to each car as it's searched."

"I'll start retrieving keys from the people over here."

"Are we dealing with one or more people?"

"I don't know. Maybe Klein is just pulling the strings. Hutton certainly seems to have been the kind of guy you could pay to stir things up."

"Then Klein killed him. Maybe."

"That might be his plan. Use people and then kill them so they can't run their mouths. Again, with someone like Hutton, you'd have to figure that sooner or later he'd run his mouth. Either to a cop when he got caught or to some other lowlife."

"Where's this get us?"

"We'll know more after we search the cars in the parking lot," I said, trying to think positively.

Forty-five minutes later, we'd looked inside every trunk and in the back of any pickup with a topper or other covering. Everyone was soaked and exhausted.

"I don't see how she can still be here," I finally admitted to Dad as I tried my best to dry myself with a towel. "I guess I was wrong about the video footage. Maybe he drove over the curb, or Captain Bennett's right and he walked away with her. He could have had his car parked somewhere else nearby. I'd just hoped…" I stopped and swallowed hard. "I'm going over to talk to Charley."

My phone rang before I headed back out into the storm again.

"The good news is, Luke'll live," Darlene said when I answered. "The bad news is he's not likely to remember anything."

"Judging by the video footage, he probably didn't see anything," I said, then told Darlene about Cara.

"Damn it! We can't get back. They've made it very clear that Hondo will lose his job if he drives his ambulance anywhere until the all-clear is given. I don't think we could get back anyway. There are a lot of trees down already. We had to drive around a couple on our way into Tallahassee."

"Stay put. If you have access to a computer, then do what Luke was trying to do and find any connections between our victims and Blake Klein. Or just between Lynch and Hutton. You know the routine. Common places, people, jobs— anything that links them."

"Will do. I'm sure I can find a computer here at the hospital and I won't have to worry about losing power." She paused. "Cara will be fine."

"Thanks."

I shrugged into a raincoat, though I didn't know why I was bothering. I was already soaked through and I really didn't give a damn about being wet. Outside, the parking lot and street were full of obstacles. Streams of moving water, fallen branches and other debris frequently blocked my path. I walked carefully, relying on the flashlight and hoping that no one else was out there waiting to attack me in the middle of the tempest.

I swiped my keycard at the back door and cautiously

entered the sheriff's office.

"Oh, it's you," Charley said. He was standing near the door, holding a ten-pound dumbbell from the workout room.

"That would do the job," I told him, indicating the dumbbell. He lowered it.

"Sorry. I just got a bit nervy after you all left." His eyes shifted right and left as we talked. I took another look at the dumbbell and thought about the man who'd struck Luke with the lead pipe.

"I want to ask you some questions."

"About what?"

"Let's go in the break room and sit down," I said, wanting him on the other side of a table while we talked. I didn't really think he was a viable suspect, but my job wasn't to speculate before gathering evidence.

Charley grabbed a Coke from the refrigerator, offered me one that I refused, then sat down across from me.

"Where were you before Luke Garner was attacked?"

"Back here. I was double-checking the generator. Making sure that the ventilation was clear and the fuel tank was still full. I'm a little OCD about that sort of thing."

I watched Charley as he talked. His eyes were focused and he was concentrating as he talked, obviously going over the timeline in his head. I thought again about the dumbbell. In a head-to-head struggle, I thought Charley would be a formidable opponent.

"Did you hear anything?"

"This building is pretty well insulated. I didn't hear a sound or know that anything was wrong until you came back to the maintenance room. You can't seriously think I would beat a man half to death." He stared at me, his expression hard to read. Was he frustrated? Angry? Or was he only pretending to be offended?

"We're just trying to get to the bottom of all of this. Have you ever heard of a man named Blake Klein?"

"Klein? Not that I know of. Can you give me any

context?"

I pulled out my phone and did a quick search on the Internet. In under a minute, I had pulled up a news article about the murders on Pelican Island. The article included a good picture of Blake Klein. I expanded the picture so that Charley wouldn't be able to see any of the article and showed it to him.

"This is a picture of him," I said. "Do you recognize him? Have you seen him anywhere around here in the last month?"

"No, I don't think so. I'm pretty good with faces. I think I'd remember him."

"His hair might be longer or shorter or a different color."

"I get that. Still haven't seen him."

Next I pulled up a picture of Cara. When I showed him the phone this time, his expression changed.

"I recognize her. I've seen her around. Don't know her name."

"Her name is Cara Laursen. She was working over at the emergency management center. But she's been missing for more than two hours."

The last bit of irritation seemed to fall away from his expression. "You're kidding?"

"No. It was around the same time as the attack on Luke. Maybe before, maybe after."

"Are you telling me there's some madman stalking us? It was bad enough when that guy was attacked. Now you're telling me someone else has gone missing?"

"When was the last time you saw Cara?"

"I don't know. I'm not even sure where I've seen her."

"Do you have any pets?"

"I had a dog. He passed away a couple months ago." Then he snapped his fingers. "She works at the vet! I remember her now. Really sweet girl. Always seemed glad to see Rowdy. Of course, he was a great dog." He stopped when he remembered why I was asking about her. "Shit."

"Now think. Have you ever seen this person?" I asked,

showing him one of the photos of Stevie Ray Hutton's body.

"Is he dead?"

"Look at his face. Do you recognize him?"

"Hard to tell from that picture. Maybe. Trouble is, there've been so many different people around here the last couple of weeks, what with the construction company getting ready to start on the addition and then the preparations for the storm. Your dad brought a whole group of people through the place a couple days ago. I think they were with the emergency management team. I'm just saying…" Charley seemed genuinely frustrated that he couldn't be more help.

"Keep thinking. Anything you can remember that stood out over the last couple of weeks could be important," I said.

My phone started ringing in my hand. I glanced at the caller ID and answered, "Hi, Pete."

"You owe me, buddy," he said cheerily and, for a moment, an insanely optimistic part of my brain thought he had found Cara. But since he didn't even know she was missing, I chastised myself for being an idiot.

"Why?" was my lame response.

"I found Hitdawg."

"How'd you get him?"

"He came into the shelter. Seems he'd been hiding in some hole he'd dug by his house down in the Ditch and almost drowned when the creek started rising. He and a woman came dragging in here like drowned rats. He gave some false name, but your buddy is pretty distinctive."

"Cara's been abducted," I said abruptly, then told him what we knew.

"I wish I could get over there," he said, his voice dark.

"Me too."

"Do you think Hitdawg might know anything?"

"Probably not. But I guess it's possible."

"Well, we'll see. I'm going to spend the evening with him."

I filled him in on what little we knew about Stevie Ray

Hutton, as well as the attack on Luke—anything that I thought might help him with his interrogation of Hitdawg. Of course, with Pete, subjects often didn't know they were being interrogated. He could be deceptive. He sometimes came across as a big, good-natured goofball, but most people soon learned that his unprofessional manner concealed a sharp mind that could focus on a goal like a Golden Retriever on a tennis ball.

"I'll call you if I learn anything," he said, and I promised to let him know if there were any developments concerning Cara.

I put my phone down and turned my attention back to Charley.

"I've got some things I need to check out. Keep an eye on the office."

"No problem. The doors are all locked and the windows boarded up. Someone tries to get in, there'll be time to sound the alarm," he said.

I thought how ironic it was that the sheriff's office didn't have an alarm system. But then why would it? Normally it was occupied 24/7. Since any number of people might need to get into the building at any time, you'd have to give the code out to hundreds of people and that would just defeat the purpose of a security code. Dad had upgraded the locks on the doors to keycard access so we could all come and go when we needed to. If someone was fired, then all they had to do was deactivate their card.

Unfortunately, the front door had obviously been left unlocked when everyone was heading out to storm assignments, the disruption to everyone's normal routine leaving things undone. The blame would fall on the front desk sergeant. I couldn't remember who'd been manning the desk that afternoon. Of course, a small voice in the back of my head reminded me, it was possible that Charley had unlocked the door.

Shaking off that thought, I went to Shantel's office and grabbed paper coveralls, a mask and gloves, then headed down the hall to the conference room.

I suited up and reached for the door handle. I shouldn't have been going in and rummaging through the scene before Shantel or someone from her crew had had a chance to process it, but I thought of Cara and opened the door anyway. If there was even a slim chance that something Luke had been working on could help find Cara, then I was willing to take any chance.

When we'd rushed in to save Luke, the focus had been on him and his injuries. Even without Luke's body on the floor, the room still showed signs of the fierce nature of the attack. I used my phone to take pictures of the scene so there would be a record of what it had looked like before I started poking around.

After documenting as much as I could, I called Darlene. "How's Luke?"

"Hanging in there. 'Critical' is the word they're using. You know how it is. Until the doctors have had a chance to do all their tests and look at the results, they aren't going to commit to a prognosis. Anything on Cara?"

"Not yet and it's driving me crazy. So I'm looking over everything in the conference room now."

"I've been working on background for Lynch and Hutton. I'd been curious what Luke had pulled up."

"The laptop is open." I tapped a button and a screen pulled up. "Luckily, he'd plugged it in so there's still plenty of power. It's open to his email. Looks like he sent some inquiries about Hutton's time in prison."

"I've got some of that. He spent most of his incarcerated life in Georgia. North Florida Correctional was his lone experience with the Florida prison lifestyle. It's only thirty miles from Pelican Island."

"Reading Luke's email, he was asking for a list of Hutton's visitors. No answer yet. They're dealing with the storm down there too. Even if they weren't, this kind of public information request would be pretty low on the priority list."

"Unless you know someone," Darlene said.

My brain took a minute to catch up to what she was suggesting. "Captain Bennett," I finally said.

"He runs in those circles. If I remember correctly, he spent about ten years working for Florida corrections."

"I'll call you right back," I said, hanging up and calling Dad. I didn't want Bennett to even hesitate to call in some favors. Coming from me, he might have to think about it. Coming from Dad, not so much.

"On it," was all Dad said.

I called Darlene back.

"Did you tell your dad that you're mucking around in an unprocessed crime scene?"

"You know, for once I'm not worried about him being mad or disappointed in me."

"I don't think you have any reason to be. Your dad's a no-bullshit kind of guy when someone's life is on the line. That's one of the reasons I was happy to come over to the sheriff's office from the police department. Chief Maxwell is smart and professional, but what he lacks is the confidence to charge ahead when action is called for. If I was in trouble, I'd want to know that your dad was on the job." She paused for a moment before adding, "And you too, of course."

"Finger coming at you," I said without malice. "I'm looking at Luke's notes. He's done a pretty thorough timeline for Rudy Lynch. Naturally, he's been working on this since he got the original email suggesting Klein's involvement." I scanned down the timeline that ran a full two pages, then did the same for a shorter list Luke had made for Hutton that afternoon. "There's a lot to cross-check here, but one interesting thing I see is that Lynch went to Valdosta State University for a year. Looking at Hutton's timeline, it's possible they were both in Georgia at the same time. Hutton was even out of prison for part of it."

"Georgia's a big state."

"Hutton was doing some outpatient time at the state hospital in Thomasville, which is only about forty miles from

Valdosta."

"Still likely it's a coincidence. There have been plenty of cases where a woman was found murdered and it turned out that several killers and rapists had lived nearby, but that none of them were involved in her death. Coincidences can drive you crazy if you let them."

"I'm getting a call from Dad. Call you back later," I said.

"Some of the guys over here have come up with an idea," Dad said. "You'll want to hear this."

"What is it?"

"I think you should come back and hear it from them," he said in a voice that told me not to question him.

I looked around. What was I really learning from this mess? "Okay, give me ten minutes."

CHAPTER FIFTEEN

I went to find Charley. "I'm going back over to the center. Use the radio if you need help."

"I hope you find her. Anything I can do, just let me know." He sounded sincere.

I took a deep breath and opened the door into the gale. Holding on to the door handle, I was literally pulled outside as the wind slammed the door all the way out and against the wall. It was pitch black and I couldn't hear anything above the wind. I had to throw my full weight into it to get the door closed again. Branches and debris flew by, coming out of the darkness and passing quickly through the beam of my flashlight. I didn't have to be a meteorologist to know that I was in the middle of a hurricane. Between the wind and the water flooding the street, I slipped a few times getting across to the emergency management center.

As soon as I came through the door, a woman I knew from county administration handed me a towel. Water sloshed out of my shoes as I walked over to where Dad, Freddy Kimble and Corporal Jerry Franks were standing together with serious expressions on their faces.

"What's going on?" I asked.

"Our cousin raises hunting dogs," Freddy blurted, which

seemed like a non sequitur.

"Freddy and I are cousins," Jerry explained. "One of our other cousins, Mort Simpson, raises the best hunting dogs in the state. Bar none. Mort has this one dog that can hunt anything."

I thought I knew where this was going, but I didn't see how this was urgent considering the current strength of the storm.

"Are you saying that his dog could track Cara?"

"I know he can," Freddy said.

At the same time, Jerry said, "Absolutely. Mort loves to show this dog off on hunting trips. You can hide a hundred-dollar bill in a thousand acres and that dog will sniff your scent on it."

"A hunting dog isn't a bloodhound."

"Notch is better than any bloodhound I've ever seen," Freddy said.

"Notch?"

"He got his ear caught on some barbed wire when he was a puppy," Jerry said.

I didn't know what to say. I didn't want to turn them down; they were so earnest. But once the storm cleared, we'd be able to bring in a ton of resources, including tracking dogs from several different agencies.

"We can be back with him in an hour, tops," Jerry said.

I was touched both by their offer and their insanity.

"Out there. Now?" I wanted to tell them to go. Anything that had a chance of getting to Cara was worth the effort. But in reality, could I risk their lives? "I want to tell you yes, but seriously, do you think Notch will work in this kind of weather?"

"I lost five hundred dollars when that dog found a set of keys I dropped in one of the worst storms I've ever seen," Freddy said. "That was two years ago. We'd been out hunting, and I lost a key-ring with three keys on it. I'd hiked over three hundred acres and they could have been anywhere. Storm came up, real thunder-boomer. I'd been out there all weekend and I just wanted to go home. Mort asked me if it was worth five hundred dollars to get my keys. Hell yeah, it was. An hour later, that dog found my keys in rain as hard as this."

"How far away is he?" I couldn't believe that I was seriously considering this.

"He's about five miles east of town."

"There's going to be trees down."

"I don't think it will be too bad once we're out of town," Jerry said. "The road has a wide shoulder. It's mostly Florida Pines land out there, and they clear-cut half of it three years ago and a bunch more this summer. There aren't a lot of trees to fall over."

"What about powerlines?"

"We can talk Ray into going along."

At the sound of his name, Ray Alverez looked over at us. "Anything I can do to help," he said, though I wondered if he realized what he was volunteering for.

I looked at Dad.

"I'm not going to tell them no," he said.

I was torn. One part of me argued for it, while another voice told me this was madness and Cara would not want others to risk their lives for her. If there was a guarantee that Notch the *wunderhund* would be able to find her, then the decision would be a no-brainer. But if Cara had been carried off to a car parked nearby, then Notch was only going to lead us to a spot on the pavement where her scent disappeared and the whole effort would just be a dangerous waste of time.

"Let's go," I finally said.

"You need to stay here," Dad snapped. As soon as I heard his voice, I recognized it from childhood. He was speaking as a father, not as the sheriff.

"I have to go," I told him and our eyes met.

After a long moment, he nodded and said, "Be careful."

"We'll be back as soon as we can."

Freddy turned to the other side of the room. "Ray! Grab

your shit and let's go!" I saw Ray raise his hand in acknowledgement. "We'll meet you out at Jerry's truck," Freddy yelled, then turned to me. "Jerry's driving."

When we got to the truck, I couldn't help but grin as I remembered what Jerry drove to work every day. It was a monster truck that stood about three feet off the ground with bright red flames streaking down both sides and the words *Burning Love* printed across the tailgate.

"Damn good thing you put these steps on," Freddy said, as he hoisted his hefty bulk up into the back of the crew cab.

"You don't have to go, Freddy," Jerry said.

"Hell yeah, I do. And I want to be there when you tell that wife of yours that you drove around in the middle of a hurricane. She's going to beat your ass." He laughed hard from deep down in his ample gut.

Ray came out a minute later, carrying a large duffel bag. Freddy grabbed the bag and Ray pulled himself into the back beside him. I grabbed shotgun next to Jerry.

With the electricity out, the drive through town was eerie. Even with the extra light bars Jerry had installed across the top of the truck, the lights could only cut a dozen feet through the pouring rain. Jerry gripped the steering wheel tightly, swerving to avoid signs, trashcans and various other items that had escaped people's yards.

He had to navigate around two fallen trees before we reached the outskirts of town. Once we were out on the rural roads, there were fewer manmade objects to avoid and more tree branches. We'd almost made it to the road that led to their cousin's house when Jerry slammed on the brakes in front of a pine tree that completely blocked the road.

"Don't get out yet," Ray said. He took a flashlight out of his bag and shined it to the right side of the road where the powerlines ran. "Looks like it just missed them. We're lucky the tree and the lines were on opposite sides of the road."

Jerry got out and pulled a twenty-inch chainsaw from the back of his truck. As he cut, the rest of us moved sections of the tree to the side of the road and it was clear in short order. Completely drenched, we climbed back into the truck.

Ten minutes later, we pulled up in front of a charming log home with its interior lights blazing. Ray waited in the truck while the rest of us sloshed our way onto the porch. The door opened before we could knock.

"Come in," said a short, lean man in his fifties. He stuck his hand out to me. "I'm Mort."

"Larry."

"That's Notch," Mort said, pointing to a leggy hound dog curled up on a rug in the middle of the living room. He lifted his head when Mort said his name.

Mort's wife came into the living room, carrying cups of coffee. "Mort got the generator going. Here," she said, handing us warm mugs. "If you need cream, let me know. I added sugar already. Y'all will need all the energy you can get. Is it true about Cara?" she asked me.

I was a little surprised that she seemed to know her. "Yes."

"She is so sweet to all our animals when we take them to Dr. Barnhill's. If anyone can find her, Notch can."

The dog got up and came over to sit next to the woman. She gave his head a good rub, then said, "Let me get you all some towels." She left for a minute and came back with two handfuls of towels, handing them out to us.

"I'm ready when you are," Mort said. "Notch." The dog trotted over to stand next to Mort with an alert expression on his face.

"Wait," his wife said and hurried back into the kitchen, coming out with a couple of thermoses and giving them to Jerry and Freddy. "Be careful."

Mort put a radio collar and orange vest on Notch, then grabbed a small satchel from beside the door and we headed back out into the storm.

There wasn't a lot of spare room in the truck and Notch was sandwiched between me and Jerry on the front seat. Jerry drove with intense concentration, at one point having to wrestle back control of the vehicle as a strong gust of wind blew us into the oncoming lane. The only advantage to driving around during a hurricane was that there weren't many other people stupid enough to do the same.

"What do you think happened to Cara?" Mort asked me.

"We know that someone grabbed her. We've searched all the cars in the parking lot, so we're pretty sure she's not there. I've gone through all the security camera footage that we have and I can't see how someone could have driven out of the lot without being caught on camera. That means they probably walked off the property. If Notch can lead us to where they went once they left the emergency management center, that could go a long way toward finding her," I said.

"Who would do that to such a nice girl like her?"

I couldn't answer. My mind couldn't accept that she was lost, but finding her was the only thing I could think about.

"Notch will need something with her scent on it."

"Won't be a problem," I said, unconsciously reaching into my pocket and clutching the heart pendant, even though I knew it wasn't a good option. A piece of clothing would have been better. Cara always kept a light jacket in her car.

Just before we got to the city limits, there was a power pole down across the road. The lines had been snapped by an oak tree, its trunk still smoking from a lightning strike.

"We don't need to deal with this," Ray said. "Back up and take the first left. It curves and leads back into town."

Everything was fine until the road Ray had directed us to descended into a low area that was now completely flooded. It was impossible to tell how deep it was.

"No worries. I've got this," Jerry said, and started through the water.

"I don't think that's a good idea," Freddy said, but by then it was too late.

The water was above the bumper. Since the truck was jacked up about three feet, that meant the floodwaters had to be almost five feet deep. The swift current was enough to push the heavy vehicle, making it feel more like a boat than a truck.

Just as my mind was starting to run through escape options, we all felt the tires hit firm ground and the truck began to rise out of the water. We breathed deep signs of relief and I slapped Jerry on the back in thanks.

A few minutes later, we parked at the emergency management center. There was a smattering of applause as we came in and Notch got a little attention before we huddled in a corner to discuss the best way to handle the search.

"Normally, I'd just turn Notch loose," Mort said, "but I'm not comfortable doing that in this kinda weather. Besides, you figure we're searching a pretty small area to start with, right?"

"Yes. The parking lot first and hopefully Notch will be able to tell where the person took her from there," I said, trying to disassociate my mind from the fact we were searching for Cara. If I thought of her as I would any other victim, then I might be able to keep from being overwhelmed by panic and dread.

"Okay, then. You get me something with her scent on it and Notch and I will go to work."

I nodded and headed back outside to Cara's car, glad I had a copy of the key on my key-ring. As soon as I stuck my head through the door, I was overwhelmed by the familiar scents that reminded me of her. My attempt to quell my own emotions failed and I felt nauseated, thinking of Cara in the hands of some cruel monster. I took several deep breaths, then grabbed her jacket from the back seat and stuffed it into a plastic bag.

Back in the center, I handed the jacket to Mort while Notch walked around on his leash, wagging his tail. I had seen trained search-and-rescue dogs do some impressive feats of tracking, but I wasn't too confident that this nondescript hound could find anything in the driving rain and wind.

"The sustained winds are seventy-two miles an hour," Dad said, bending down and scratching Notch's ears.

"If Mort and Notch are up to it…" I said, raising my eyebrows.

"I ain't sayin' we've been in worse, but I think we can do this," Mort said.

"I'm not betting any money against Notch," Jerry said.

Mort had on a raincoat and farm hat, as though either one of them was going to help him stay dry.

"You better nail that hat on," Freddy told him.

Mort looked at him, then took a handkerchief out of his pocket and wrapped it over the hat and under his chin.

"You're crazy," Freddy said good-naturedly.

I turned on my flashlight. "Ready?"

"Let's do this," Mort said. He let Notch smell Cara's jacket. The dog began to bounce up and down, tugging on the leash. "Sorry, boy, but I'm not letting you go," Mort said, then nodded to me. I swung the door open.

Notch stepped out into the storm without hesitation. The wind snapped his ears back while he pulled Mort into the blackness and noise of Marcy's fury.

I tried to stay on the windward side of Notch in order to block any debris that might come whipping by in the wind. He kept his nose to the ground, his head working back and forth. *With all this water and wind, how can he possibly follow a trail?* I thought, shining my light just in front of the dog so that Mort could see Notch and anything on the ground in front of them.

Notch, with ears flapping and eyes squinting, seemed to have found some sort of trail to follow. To my surprise, it led toward the front of the parking lot facing the sheriff's office instead of off into one of the neighborhoods near the center. We had checked the trunks of all the cars in this area and had found nothing. I didn't know what it meant that Notch was taking us out closer to the main road. The working security cameras *did* have a blind spot in the middle of the parking lot, so it was theoretically possible to cross the main street without being caught on either camera. Still, how bold would the person have had to be to drag a woman across a major road, even if the traffic had been light due to the storm?

Notch suddenly stopped and turned, working in circles.

"He's lost the scent!" Mort yelled to me.

My stomach dropped as I realized I had put more hope into Notch and his abilities than I would have wanted to admit.

Even through the sheets of water, I could see Notch's frustration as he tried and failed to find the trail. He stopped and lifted his head. Turning, he sniffed a couple of the surrounding vehicles, looking a bit confused.

I shined my flashlight around. We were next to the small SUV with the canoe on the roof. I remembered Darlene pointing it out and commenting that having a boat was the right idea. The canoe was upside down on the roof racks and I could see a green tarp filling the underside of the canoe. I'd seen people pack for a canoe trip by putting the canoe on the roof and then using it like a cargo carrier. I assumed that's what this person had done.

I passed my light over the roof of the SUV one more time and saw it. Between a couple of grooves in the roof's design and directly under the canoe was something shiny. I got closer, my heart beating faster. The second I realized it was part of the chain that had held Cara's heart pendant, everything fell into place.

"Help me!" I screamed at Mort, and began trying to undo the straps that held the canoe to the roof. My clammy hands weren't doing a very good job. Mort tied Notch's leash to his belt so that he could help, and I handed the flashlight to him so I could use both hands. I could just hear Notch barking excitedly over the screaming wind.

The straps finally fell apart and, awkwardly, we turned and let the canoe slide down the hood of the car. We eased it to the ground as best we could before I started ripping at the rope that was holding the tarp together. In seconds I felt a hand, cold and wet, and I started tearing even more frantically at the ropes and duct tape. Finally, I ripped the green fabric away and saw Cara's face. There was tape over her eyes and mouth, but at least the bastard had left her nose uncovered. I pulled the tape from her mouth and she spit water into my face. I thanked God as I pulled the rest of the tape from her eyes, even as she fought against me lethargically.

Her eyes were wild in the glare of the flashlight. I hugged her to me as I pulled her out of the canoe. Notch was dancing a crazy jig beside me as Mort held his leash in what seemed like a wild dream. I ran toward the center, still trailing ropes and tape in a flying tangle behind me. Mort opened the door and I fell to the floor, cradling Cara against me, in front of a crowd of people.

Dad was beside me in an instant, one hand on my shoulder and another on Cara's forehead. "Where was she?" he asked, then yelled, "Get Dr. Patrick!"

The words were barely out of his mouth before a crowd of people surrounded us with blankets and towels. Dr. Patrick pushed his way through the well-meaning group and got on his knees next to where I held Cara against me.

He felt for her pulse. "Everybody get back," he said, grabbing a blanket from the nearest person and laying it over the top of her. "Someone bring a cup of warm tea."

To me, he said, "Her pulse is strong and steady," as he retrieved a stethoscope from an orange medical bag he'd pulled from somewhere. "But she's in shock and her body temperature is low."

I felt Cara's hand grab onto mine tightly for the first time. "Larry, what's happening?" she asked weakly.

"Move around here," Dr. Patrick told me, shifting so that he could hold Cara's head and touch it gently. "There's a light contusion on the back of her head, but I don't think it's serious."

"You're okay now," I told her, grasping her ice-cold hands in mine.

Someone brought a cup of tea and handed it to Dad, who hadn't left my side. "When she's feeling better, she can take a warm shower in the jail's locker room," he suggested.

"That would be a good idea," Dr. Patrick said. "She'll need someone to go with her and make sure she doesn't fall. She's not going to be very steady on her feet for a few hours."

"We can get her some clean clothes and hot food too," Captain Bennett said. I hadn't seen him come in to the center, but now he was smiling down at us.

"Okay, this is embarrassing," Cara said hoarsely, trying to joke as she took the mug of tea and sipped it. "I don't understand what's going on."

At that moment, I didn't care if she couldn't remember anything about what had happened or the person who'd attacked her. As much as I wanted to catch the son of a bitch, that could come later. Right then, I just basked in the joy of having Cara with me. I whispered another prayer of thanks before admitting to myself how scared I'd been that I'd lost her. I realized then that losing her would be more than I could bear.

I pulled the heart pendant, still in its evidence bag, out of my pocket and showed it to her. Cara reached for it and we cupped it in both of our hands. "Someone attacked and abducted you," I said, finally allowing myself to feel the anger I'd tried to suppress as we searched for her.

"Who?" she asked, echoing the question that was now running over and over in my head.

"I'm going to find out," I promised and leaned down to kiss her.

CHAPTER SIXTEEN

Half an hour later, Cara was feeling well enough to shower and change into dry clothes. Melvina Hollis, a supervisor with the road department, offered to go with her and make sure she didn't fall. I was reluctant to let her out of my sight and only let go of her hand after Melvina assured me she'd keep Cara safe.

I watched them leave, then pulled Dad aside. "Whoever did this is here," I told him firmly.

"I agree," he said, surprising me. "I think pressing forward with this investigation makes sense. According to the National Hurricane Center and the state emergency management team, we have at least five more hours before we can start sending teams out to do assessments and respond to requests for assistance. I'd like to know who the rat in the cornfield is before that."

"Means, motive and opportunity."

"Means is any able-bodied individual. That rules out a few of the folks in the center. Motive?"

"I've been racking my brain over that one, but I keep coming back to Blake Klein. Can we really be seeing some sort of orchestrated attempt at revenge?"

"Thinking about what he was doing on Pelican Island, it

doesn't seem that far off from his MO. He could even be blackmailing one of the people in this room."

"And he either bought or blackmailed Stevie Ray Hutton into performing the armed robberies. But why?"

"Either just for the money, or maybe he thought it might give him an opportunity to get to you. Or both. Two birds with one stone," Dad suggested.

We were off in a corner of the basketball-court-sized room, talking low enough that no one could overhear us. I looked around the room. "What sort of hold could he possibly have on someone to coerce them into attacking a woman and leaving her in the middle of a hurricane? Dr. Patrick said she could have died from shock or exposure if she'd been left out there during the entire storm."

"What sort of tie have you found between Hutton and Klein?" Dad asked.

"All we know at the moment is that he had one of Klein's cards in his pocket," I said, then a wave of guilt rolled over me as I realized I hadn't yet called Pete or Darlene to tell them that Cara was safe. I texted Darlene first and then called Pete.

"We found Cara," I said as soon as he answered the phone. "She's okay."

"Thank God!" Pete said and I could hear the intense relief in his voice. "I've got to let Sarah know. She could tell I was upset about something when I called her earlier and she wormed the information out of me."

"Before you do that, did you find out anything useful from Rufus?" I asked.

"You mean my homie Hitdawg? Yeah, he coughed up some things he'd forgotten to mention the first couple of times he was questioned. Number one on the Hitdawg liar list is the fact that he had met Hutton before, and even suspected that's who robbed him."

"Why the hell did he lie about that?" I asked angrily, even though I knew that lying was standard operating procedure for drug dealers.

"My guess would be out of fear. He said Hutton was too crazy to deal with."

"I actually believe him. So where had he met him before and does he think Hutton was working for someone else?"

"Hutton just showed up at his place one day to buy drugs. However, Hitdawg thinks he wasn't really that interested in the drugs. Before the deal had even taken place, Hutton was asking him how much he paid for the drugs he sold and was he satisfied with the quality and quantity that he got. Hitdawg isn't an idiot. His provider would gladly cut off intimate parts of him if he even suspected that Hitdawg was thinking about doing business with another distributor. He told Hutton he got the best and got all that he could sell before he sold him what he wanted and told him not to come back again."

"Did he think Hutton came back to rob him 'cause he was pissed at him?" I asked.

"Exactly. But get this. Hutton told him he'd be sorry that he didn't sign up to do business with him because they were going to have a bumper crop of good shit. That's supposedly a direct quote."

"*They*? So Hutton was working with someone. That makes some sense. Did his partner kill him? Or was it one of the people he robbed like we suspected in the first place? And was dumping the body at Hitdawg's place a personal attack on him?"

"'Dawg doesn't think so. He said everyone loves him, so why would they throw the body in front of his house? While I don't think he's as beloved as he thinks he is, he does have a point that it doesn't make much sense. The murderer was taking a huge risk that he'd be seen."

"True. It's much safer to dump a body out in the woods. Around here, it might be years or never before a body is found. Particularly the body of someone like Hutton who no one would be particularly motivated to hunt for. So whoever killed him had to have a reason to dump the body where they did."

"Think we're circling back to your friend Klein?" Pete asked.

"Maybe. Maybe he did it, or had it done, as a way to send a message to me," I said, trying to wrap my head around the idea.

"Makes sense. He knows that you or someone close to you is going to be in charge of the investigation and will find the card with his name on it. That gets back to you and, bongo bingo, message delivered."

"Then he gets someone to abduct Cara," I said, still trying to get all of the differently shaped pegs to fit in the corresponding holes. "Something just doesn't add up. Why not just kill Cara? Or Dad? Or even me? It doesn't make sense. But right now, Klein's motivation doesn't really matter… Whether he hired someone to do this or someone did it on their own, the person who abducted Cara is here." I looked again at all the people in the room. Some of them I knew well, but others I'd barely met.

I thanked Pete for his help and hung up, turning back to Dad, who'd been listening.

"You heard most of that. Anyone here could have a motive if Klein is backstage pulling the strings. In some ways, that's the only thing that makes sense. Otherwise, we have to figure out who has a grudge against me or Cara. Looking around this room, there's no one that we even know that well except you… and I'm pretty sure you didn't do it," I said grimly.

"Valid points. I always like to use motives to develop suspects, but there's just not enough information in this case."

"Opportunity," I said.

Dad nodded. "While you were out surfing the storm to get Notch, I worked on a timeline. I've got the number of people who had an opportunity to nab Cara down to six. My list is even more valid now that we know they didn't have to be gone very long."

"Just long enough to follow Cara outside, club her over

the head, wrap her up in a tarp and stuff her in a canoe. Getting her in the canoe wouldn't have been easy. Honestly, if she was any larger it would be close to impossible."

Dad looked at his list. "Then I can mark off two people for not being physically capable of getting her into the canoe."

"Who does that leave?"

"Dr. Greg Patrick, Floyd Krueger, Freddy Kimble and Brian Atkins. I'm leaving out Jake Middleton, who weighs less than Cara, and Woodrow Warner, who isn't in very good health."

"What about the people working in the jail?"

"Captain Bennett checked the security logs. No one left the building during the time Cara went missing."

"We have to include Charley Wright," I said. "He could have run from across the street and no one would have seen him."

"Agreed. He's smart and certainly strong enough."

"What about the SUV the canoe was strapped to?"

"I ran the plates. Stolen. I've got Bennett checking the security cameras. We should be able to see when it was left in the lot. But since it's so far from the building, I doubt we'll get a good look at who left it."

"I think I might know. Baggie saw Hutton in the area two days ago. He could have left it."

"It's registered to someone down in Panama City. Which makes sense. If you planned to leave a stolen vehicle in a public lot for a couple of days, you wouldn't want it to have been stolen from someone local."

"Sounds like some serious planning went into all of this."

"There's even that game camera on your property," Dad reminded me.

"Why would someone go to all this trouble?"

"We did screw Klein out of everything he'd built. Took all his money, or at least all that we could find, and left him with an identity that he can't use. I'd be pretty angry."

"All true," I said, wondering if Klein was living out some

sort of supervillain revenge plot. If anyone was up to the challenge, it would be him. "Any thoughts on who we should question first?"

"Your case, your choice. We have to go easy and be explicit about what we're doing. And we should definitely record the interviews. These are pretty unusual circumstances. If someone says something incriminating, or just something we want to use in court later, we don't want it thrown out because of the methods and timing of the questioning."

"Agreed."

"We can use Sergeant Bevin's office," Dad suggested. Bevin was the coordinator of all visits to the jail and had been given his own office so that, if there were ever any problems or questions, he could talk to the lawyer, family members or friends without risking an altercation in the reception area. His office would be fully equipped with recording equipment.

"Let's take Brian Atkins first," I said. "Dr. Patrick wanted to check Cara over again after she'd had a chance to get cleaned up and eat something. We'll take him next, if he's free."

Dad went over and explained the situation to Brian, who appeared to take the news that he was a suspect well enough. I followed them through the door that connected the annex to the jail, and Dad used a security card to get us into the locked part of the building where Bevin's office was located.

The office was roomier than I had expected. It held a desk, four chairs and a museum's worth of baseball memorabilia. Many of the team photos included a younger Bevin wearing a mitt and a smile. We all sat together on the visitor's side of the desk.

Brian Atkins worked for the county commission as a troubleshooter. Technically, his title was Community Liaison, but everyone knew that his job was to stop the crap from rolling uphill. When a constituent complained to a commissioner, the commissioner called Brian and told him to fix it before the resident changed their mind and voted for someone else. Everyone agreed that Brian was perfect for the job. He was tall, good looking and he'd say anything to smooth over a problem. He also had a reputation for throwing other county employees under the bus. He was loved by the commission and barely tolerated by everyone else who worked for the county.

I explained to Brian that the interview was being filmed and got his consent to be questioned.

"I can't believe that anyone on the emergency management team assaulted…" He hesitated and looked at me. "Your girlfriend. Is that right?"

"Cara, yes, she's my girlfriend," I said, feeling like he was taking notes. "We're just talking to everyone that might have seen something."

"Or been involved, right?" Was he going to end every sentence with right?

"We think there's a chance this was done by someone working in the building at the time," Dad said diplomatically.

"Well, go ahead and ask me anything," Brian said, spreading his arms wide. It was easy to dislike him and equally easy to believe that he could be the county manager in a couple of years.

"We're focused on a forty-minute period between when Cara was last seen and when she was discovered missing," I said.

"According to the conversation we had earlier, you went to the bathroom and made a phone call between seven and seven-thirty," Dad said, looking at his notes.

"That's right. I called a friend and we talked for a little while before I went back into the center."

"Walk me through what you did," I said. "You went down the hall to the bathroom right before seven." The bathrooms were located in the hall that connected the emergency management annex to the jail.

"Correct."

"How long were you in the bathroom?"

"Not long. I just went there for a slash, as the British say."

"And then you made a phone call to a friend," I said, ignoring his attempt at witty banter.

"That's right."

"Where'd you make the call?"

"That's kind of funny," he said, sounding more embarrassed than amused.

Dad and I just looked at him, giving him lots of silence to fill. I thought he was going to wait us out, but after a minute he caved.

"I went into the little janitor's closet right next to the bathrooms." He spoke fast, as though we might let it slide if he said it quickly enough.

"Why did you go into the janitor's closet to make a phone call?" I put the obvious question to him.

"Why do you think? For a little privacy," he said, and a little color rose in his cheeks.

"You're a smart guy. You know what the next question is," Dad said.

"I'd rather not tell you."

"I'm sure that's true," Dad said, and he and I gave Brian the silent treatment again.

"You can stare at me all you want, but I don't have to tell you who I was talking to," he finally said, ratcheting up the attitude.

"Very true," I told him. "But it would be a lot easier if you did or, better yet, give us your phone and let us see the number and the time the call was made." I was trying to sound reasonable.

"No. I told you where I was. Do you have anyone that says I was somewhere else?" He sounded like a man who was guilty.

According to Dad, no one had seen Brian during that time, but we weren't going to tell him that.

"Is it a woman?" I asked. He just stared back at me. "Are you married?"

"Yes," he allowed.

"So you don't want your wife to find out what you were doing in a closet talking to a woman. We understand. If this goes wider, we won't be able to control what gets back to her or doesn't. But by talking now, you have a chance for us to eliminate you as a suspect. That happens and your name doesn't get brought up anymore." I spread my hands out in a *see-how-easy-it-can-be* gesture.

"I know my rights," he said, using a phrase that caused any LEO's hackles to rise. First of all, few people really did know what their rights were and, second, why bother to say it? Either exercise them or don't.

"I'm sure you do," I said, playing along. "But we aren't talking about what you can or can't do under the law. What we're talking about is what would be best for you." I almost added, "and your family," but that could have opened a can of worms that was better left closed.

"I think we're done," Brian said, but he didn't stand up.

"Fine. We'll make a note that you were uncooperative," I said.

Brian turned to Dad. "You're in a pretty tight race for reelection."

"What does that have to do with this interview?" Dad said coolly.

"I know a lot of people. I spend a bunch of my time working with community leaders," he said, letting the implications speak for themselves.

"So?" Dad wasn't taking the bait.

"Turn the cameras off."

"I don't think that would be a good idea," Dad said.

I said, "This is all pretty simple. We have months to do background on you. Right now is about giving you an opportunity to come out on top and take your name out of the running. It's really just a yes or no thing." I shrugged.

"I get that. You don't understand the situation I'm in," Brian said, giving me the eye.

I moved into his space. "I don't understand the situation

you're in? Is that what you just had the nerve to say to me? The woman I love was kidnapped. One of my friends was attacked and almost killed. But your situation is… what? More serious? More dangerous? Possibly more traumatizing?"

He blinked. Then he pulled a pen out of his pocket and reached out, taking a piece of paper off a notepad on Bevin's desk. Hunched over and blocking the camera, he wrote something on the paper. When he was done, he stood up and, like someone in a 1940s film noir, summoned us over to the corner of the room where he could stand with his back to the camera. Rolling my eyes, I went over to him. Dad didn't even bother.

Brian showed me the paper, making sure that what was written on it couldn't possibly be picked up on video. Feeling like I was being drawn into his drama, I looked at the paper. And I immediately knew that he was telling the truth and understood why he was being so cagey. I wanted to say the name out loud, but the jerk looked so terrified that I resisted the temptation.

"We'll check it out," I said sternly and added, "Discreetly. How long were you on the phone?"

Brian got extra points for pulling out his phone and showing me. It had been thirty minutes.

"Can I go now?" All the bluff and bluster were gone. He knew that we had him by the shorthairs.

"Please," I said.

As soon as he was out the door, I turned off the camera and recorder.

"Who was she?" Dad asked. He'd been around long enough to know which end of the stick was which.

"Colleen Henry," I said, and was amused to see that, for once, Dad was caught completely by surprise.

"No shit?" he said, his eyes wide. Colleen Henry was the wife of Commissioner Julian Henry, one of the county's two black commissioners. Julian owned a chain of beauty salons in the Big Bend area. In addition, he also sold beauty supplies to other salons and directly to customers. Rumor had it that he was the richest of all the county commissioners. Colleen was his third wife, a beauty that he used to show off his business products. She'd been Miss Florida ten years earlier.

"All the cloak-and-dagger stuff is understandable," I said. Then a thought occurred to me. "Of course, that's just the type of secret Blake Klein would use to blackmail someone."

"I'm still trying to get over the shock," Dad said. "Brian would be out of a job in an instant if word of that ever got out. And Colleen wouldn't be in a much better position. Julian's been divorced twice already. I doubt he'd hesitate to kick her to the curb if he found out."

"Which gives us two people that Klein could blackmail," I said. "Does it make sense for Brian to admit it now?"

"He didn't have much choice. And the phone in the closet could have been a backup alibi. He could have dialed the phone and kept the connection open the whole time he was abducting Cara."

"Colleen would have every reason in the world to go along with the plan. Even now, if we confront her, she can backup his story. Thinking about it, it's a pretty clever alibi. This area is too small for pinging off of cell towers to give him away."

"That could be why he didn't drive Cara someplace after he abducted her," Dad suggested.

"I thought I'd be able to eliminate him after seeing that piece of paper. Now I'm thinking he's moved to the number one position."

"Early days," Dad said.

My phone rang. "You told Pete first!" Darlene said without preamble.

"I texted you."

"Buddy, you better learn how to treat your partner. Good news should always be delivered in person. If you have bad news for me, take your time. Good news, though, call me and let me bask in it. How's she doing?"

I filled Darlene in on what Cara had gone through. "I was just getting ready to check on her," I said, then went on to tell her about our interview with Brian, leaving out only the part about who he was having sexy talk with. If the guy was innocent, then I didn't want to drag Colleen Henry into anything unnecessarily. Him, I couldn't care less about.

"I haven't found much more," Darlene said. "It's going to take phone calls. Asking around. After midnight during a hurricane just doesn't seem the right time. So far there aren't any obvious links between Klein, Hutton and Lynch. But I've got a couple more roads to go down."

"Here are a few more to check on," I said, and gave her the names of the four people in the center, plus Charley Wright.

"I think I remember Floyd mentioning that he used to work for one of the counties on the coast. Could be a link to Pelican Island. I'll cross-check them all with our victims and your bogeyman Klein," she said.

After we hung up, I turned to Dad. "I'm going to check on Cara. I'll bring Dr. Patrick back with me."

CHAPTER SEVENTEEN

I found Cara in a chair in the emergency management center, wearing a deputy's shirt and pants. Notch was sitting between her legs and she had her arms wrapped around him as she planted kisses on top of his head. Mort stood beside her, looking embarrassed as she thanked both of them for finding her.

I watched them for a while, happy just to be able to see her smile. Eventually, I joined them and rescued Mort, thanking him again myself before he rejoined Freddy and Jerry on the other side of the center.

"I don't think Dad is going to pay you," I kidded her, tugging on the sleeve of her shirt. "He's already got one claim of nepotism against him."

"It was this or orange coveralls."

"You made the right choice." I pulled her into a fierce hug. "How are you feeling?" I asked when I finally let her go.

"Okay right now. A little sore, and probably more sore tomorrow. Dr. Patrick wants me to go in for X-rays as soon as the storm passes." She sounded strong.

"Have you remembered anything?"

"No. I think that's why I'm not more freaked out. It's like I was here at the center, then the next thing I remember is waking up, feeling like hell with everyone standing over me. I don't think I want to remember being tied up in that canoe. I'm just glad you all saved me." Her voice broke a little and she swallowed.

"You saved yourself," I said. I dug in my pockets until I found the two-inch piece of chain that I'd pulled from the top of the SUV. "You must have dropped this from the canoe at some point."

I'd let her keep the heart pendant and she took it out of her pocket. Looking down at it, she said, "I... don't remember doing any of it."

"If the attacker had pulled it off your neck, we would have found all of it in one spot. I'm guessing that you broke the chain when you knew you were being abducted and then dropped pieces of it as you went. Most of the chain was probably washed away by the storm."

"Sorry for breaking your mom's necklace."

"I think Dad and I will forgive you. We'll get a new chain." I gave her another long hug, never wanting to let her go. Finally, I left her under Melvina's careful supervision and hunted up Dr. Patrick.

He was sitting at a table fiddling with his phone. "We've got at least three more hours of hurricane-force winds," he said when I walked up.

"Dad and I would like to ask you a few questions."

"Sure." He stood up and followed me out of the center. "I think Cara's going to be fine. Her heart rate and temperature were back to normal after she had a shower and a little something to eat."

"I appreciate you taking care of her. How bad was the blow to her head?"

"I doubt she ever completely lost consciousness. But she was badly dazed and went into shock shortly after being tied up and placed on top of the car. She also has some contusions and abrasions from being hoisted into the canoe. She should go to the hospital and get checked out as soon as it's possible, but all in all, I'd say you both were very lucky."

Dad met us at the door of Bevin's office. "Glad you were here to look after Cara," he told the doctor. "We're just working on a list of people who were unaccounted for during her abduction." Dad waved him toward a chair while explaining that this was a voluntary interview on his part and that the conversation would be recorded.

"I understand. As you know, we went over and checked on Luke together. When I was coming back, I stopped by my car."

"Why'd you go to your car?" I asked.

"To get a towel and a change of clothes. I keep a spare set in the car. As a doctor, there's always a chance of getting vomit or blood or both on your clothes. I'm not obsessive about it, but I try and maintain a certain level of hygiene," he said with small smile.

"Did anyone see you going to your car?"

"I doubt it. The storm was so bad at that point. A branch just missed me when I was coming back into the building. We've all been taking some crazy chances." He shook his head. "Who in the world is doing all of this?"

"That's what we want to know," I said plainly.

"It would have to be someone very determined and more than just a little bit crazy," Dr. Patrick said.

"Crazy. Possibly. It would help if we knew what the motive was," I said.

"You don't have any evidence?"

"Some, but it's going to take a while to test it. The question is, where will it lead? Getting back to your movements, where did you change after getting the clean clothes?"

"It was more about getting *dry* clothes. I changed in the bathroom in the center."

"Did you see anyone?"

"That guy who works for the county. Tall, good-looking guy. He was... This is going to sound strange. I probably should have mentioned it earlier, now that I think about it. He was coming out of a closet."

"When did you see him?"

"As I was going into the bathroom to change. He looked… flushed. And that's a medical observation."

"What did you do with the clothes you took off?" I asked.

"I set them down near where I've been sitting in the center," he said, then added, "They should be in the plastic bag I brought from the car."

I made a note to check on the bag.

"Did you see anything while you were outside?" Dad asked. "I know with the rain and darkness, the odds are slim."

"No. And with the wind, I couldn't hear anything either."

"What did you use for light?" I asked. These days most people would say their cell phones, but I doubted he'd used his phone in the middle of a deluge.

Dr. Patrick reached into a pocket and pulled out a small light used for examining patients. "I've got dozens of these. The drug companies hand them out like candy. It gave off just enough light for me to see the ground in front of me. If I hadn't known where my car was, I wouldn't have found it with this."

"Do you know either of these two men?" I asked, showing him pictures of Stevie Ray Hutton and Ruddy Lynch. I flipped back and forth between them on my phone.

"No. I don't think so. Though post mortem pictures don't usually do the victims justice."

"Have you ever worked near Pelican Island?" I tossed out as an afterthought.

"Work, no. But I have been down there. I worked about forty miles west of there before I came here, so we spent some weekends on the island."

"We?"

"Friends, girls, co-workers."

I gave him points for admitting he'd been there. He could have just said that he'd never been and left it at that.

"Have you ever heard of a man named Blake Klein?"

"Oh, yeah, he murdered some people on the island. Wasn't he caught or something?"

"The boat he was in wrecked and he was presumed killed," I said.

"Then why are you asking about him?" Dr. Patrick's eyes narrowed.

"There is some evidence that points toward him being involved in recent events," Dad said, deflecting the question.

We talked a little bit longer, but Dr. Patrick didn't have anything else to offer.

"The trouble with questioning intelligent suspects is that they are intelligent," I said after he'd left.

"Occasionally, they're the easiest because they're arrogant and think that cops are stupid. Of course, arrogant is on a spectrum. Compared to that ass Brian, no one would seem arrogant. The doctor was outside and he had a window of opportunity between seeing Luke off to the hospital and when you realized Cara was missing."

"Yeah, but I'm not sure I buy it. Besides, he'd have to be in league with whoever attacked Luke. According to your timeline, he was here in the center when that attack happened."

I left to get one of the other two suspects and caught up with the doctor as he was entering the center.

"Dr. Patrick, let me see those clothes, if you don't mind."

"Of course."

I followed him to where he'd been sitting earlier and, sure enough, there was a heavy-duty plastic shopping bag from a Tallahassee shoe store lying beside his chair. He picked it up and handed it to me. Inside were some very wet clothes and nothing else. His story checked out, so I handed the bag back to him.

I turned to see Freddy Kimble chatting with Mort. Notch was sprawled out on the floor next to Mort's feet, looking very content.

"Freddy, could Dad and I have a word with you?" I asked, and explained what we wanted.

"Ask me questions? What about?" he said a little louder than I thought was necessary.

"Just some routine questions. Dad has compiled a list of some folks that couldn't be accounted for during the time that Cara was abducted."

"What are you saying?" His eyes had hardened. I'd never seen Freddy be anything but open and friendly. I knew that Dad had almost considered taking him off of the list because of his age and the physicality of the crime, but we both knew that Freddy did quite a bit of tough manual labor as part of his job with public works. I looked at his muscled arms and thought that he would certainly be capable of hoisting someone as small as Cara onto the top of a car.

"We're just talking to people, that's all. We're going to be cooped up here for a few more hours. It's important to get a jump on the investigation."

"Save yourself some time and go question someone else, 'cause I didn't have anything to do with hurting that poor woman. Why would I have helped go get Notch here if I had done that to her? Wouldn't make any sense."

"And you know how much I appreciated your help. But from a professional investigation standpoint, we have to talk with everyone who had the opportunity. If you can answer a few questions, we'll be able to eliminate you and move on," I said as patiently as I could.

"Fine. I'm telling you now I didn't have nothin' to do with her being abducted. Now you've asked and I've answered. Go talk to someone else." His eyes were hard as granite and his arms were folded tightly across his chest. He was the very picture of recalcitrant.

"Freddy, you know better than that. We need an alibi to work with."

"You don't need no alibi. I give you my word. I didn't do nothin' to her. And I'm not going to be grilled by a bunch of cops," Freddy said, becoming more irrational. *A bunch of cops? Where did he get that?* I thought.

"I can't make you talk to us, but I've got to tell you,

you're making this a lot harder than it needs to be."

"Don't care. I got my rights." Was everyone going to use that line?

"Okay," I said, puzzled by the whole conversation, and left him glaring at me from his chair.

I found Floyd Krueger sitting in front of his laptop. The laptop was on, but Floyd was off. His head was tilted to the side and he was snoring softly. I bumped the table gently.

"Huh?" he said, sitting up with a snort.

"Hey, Floyd. I was wondering if Dad and I could ask you a few questions?" I said the words slowly, giving him time to wake up and process what I was asking.

"Damn, I must have fallen asleep." He looked at his watch. "Sure. How's your girlfriend doing?"

"She'll be fine. We're in an office over there." I pointed toward the hallway.

"Yeah, okay. Questions? What about?" Floyd was still a little sluggish from his nap. "I need some water." He stood up and headed for a refreshment table against the wall.

"We're trying to establish everyone's movements during the time that Cara went missing." After Freddy's reaction, I wasn't sure what to expect from Floyd.

"Sure." He picked up a bottle of water from a huge stack and followed me down to Bevin's office.

Dad went through the recording spiel again while Floyd dropped into a chair.

"I don't know what I can tell you," he said.

"When we spoke earlier, you couldn't say for sure where you were during the time that Cara went missing. We really need you to think back and try to remember," Dad said.

"I was all over. Worked on my computer. Went to the bathroom a couple times. Ate a sandwich I brought with me. I don't know. I wasn't keeping track of when I was doing everything," he said in an absentminded professor sort of way.

I'd seen him at county commission meetings where he came across as a very smart guy who knew just about everything there was to know about zoning and planning in Adams County. However, if he was asked a personal question or something else he wasn't prepared for, he would sometimes slip into confused and sloppy behavior. I'd previously thought that he did it to stall for time or to look unassuming, but now I was beginning to think he was just one of those people who was really smart, but not very good at running their day-to-day affairs.

"Let's write things down and see if we can't come up with a timeline," I said. I found a pad of paper and a pen. "Start with when you got to the center."

"I don't know. I left the house, stopped and picked up a sandwich, then drove here. It was already raining hard when I parked. I know that," he mumbled.

"You might want to look at your phone. Maybe you got a call or messages that might jog your memory," I suggested, feeling like I was interviewing a child.

"Good idea. I'm constantly getting texts." He started scrolling through his messages and recent calls and I made a note of them on my pad. "Here's one I sent to my ex telling her that I was here and how I was going to get soaked going to the building."

"You always let your ex know where you are?" Dad asked conversationally.

"Heck, yeah. We coordinate things about our son, plus she kind of looks after me. We got divorced... four... five... a few years ago, but I couldn't make it without her. I drove her crazy when we lived together, though," he said, and I thought it was probably an understatement.

Twenty minutes later, we'd managed to cobble together a rough timeline. The only problem was that there was still a large gap during the time Cara went missing.

"Can I see your phone?" I asked.

He shrugged and handed it over to me. I looked at it. He hadn't texted anyone during that time which, looking at his messages, was unusual. From just a quick look at the phone, I'd have said he was texting someone at the rate of every ten minutes between the time he got up that morning to around midnight, except for a forty-five-minute period of time right around Cara's disappearance and Luke's attack.

"I talked to everyone in the center at the time and no one saw you. One person thought you might have gone outside. Could you have gone outside?" Dad asked as I handed the phone back to Floyd. Floyd just looked confused by the question.

I was thinking that all this was useless. First, I didn't think the guy had the organizational skills to have pulled off the two attacks and, second, I didn't think he could be considered a trustworthy witness of anything. Asking him if he saw someone or heard anything seemed ridiculous when he couldn't even remember what he was doing or where he was doing it.

"That looks right," he said when we showed him the timeline.

"So what did you do during the gap?" Dad asked.

"I... don't know," Floyd said, looking puzzled. I wondered if his parents had purposefully named him after the dimwitted barber on that old TV show with Andy Griffith.

"May I see your phone again?"

He shrugged and handed it back to me. I went back to his texts and looked at the ones he'd sent right after the gap in time. A couple were answers to ones he'd received during the gap, but he'd also sent one to someone named Sally telling her to make a note to pull the jail's blueprints.

"Would this text have anything to do with where you were during that time?" I asked him, handing him the phone.

He read the text and his face lit up like the sky on the Fourth of July. It turned out that he'd decided to kill some time by walking around the building to see if the jail matched the diagrams that the planning department had on file. He'd left his phone in the center during this time, explaining the absence of text messages.

"There are some serious discrepancies between our

online diagrams and the actual footprint of the building," he said, and then went on for another five minutes, detailing all of those discrepancies, until Dad and I had had enough and kicked him out.

"Either he's a great actor or the most personally disorganized person I've ever met," I said.

"It's him. I had to deal with him about six months ago when we were solidifying the plans for the addition on the sheriff's office. I finally just went through his PA for everything. He can draw from memory the layout of every building in the county, but he can't remember what he had for dinner or who he's supposed to meet with from minute to minute," Dad said, shaking his head.

Then I told him about Freddy's reaction when I'd asked him to meet with us.

"That's odd. I've never seen Freddy be anything but friendly and helpful."

"Do you want to try talking to him?"

"Let's do a little background first."

Dad logged into our office files through the sergeant's computer.

"He has an arrest for a DUI, which then turned into a resisting arrest. Convicted of the DUI and the resisting charge looks like it was dropped."

"I'm surprised that he was hired by the county, considering the DUI. Doesn't his job require driving county vehicles?"

"The DUI was in the early '80s when they were looked at a little differently than they are today. He was nineteen at the time. Interesting," Dad said thoughtfully. He took out his phone and dialed.

"How are you weathering the storm?" he asked the person on the other end of the line, putting the call on speaker.

"I was sleeping through it," I heard Sergeant Dill Kirby grumble. Dill was a semi-retired deputy who filled in on the front desk from time to time. Figuring Dad wasn't making a social call, he asked, "What's wrong?"

"We've had some trouble down here at the emergency management center. I have a question for you. You know Freddy Kimble in public works?"

"Sure. He's been around almost as long as me. His sister and mine are good friends. Why?"

"We're trying to clear up some questions and one of them involves Freddy. You were a deputy when he was in high school, right?"

"I'm... let's see... ten years older, roughly, so, yeah. What's this all about? Is Freddy okay?"

"He's fine. Did he get into some trouble when he was in high school, or maybe a little after?" Dad asked.

There was silence from the other end of the phone, then Dill finally asked, "Is he in trouble now?"

"That's what we're trying to figure out," Dad said honestly.

Dill sighed. "Freddy got into a bunch of it when he was a kid. You have to understand that his parents were—there's no other way to put it—worthless trash. They abused all their kids. I told you my sister is friends with his sister. Truth is, she lived with us for most of her senior year because her parents weren't providing a decent home. I suspect it was more than neglect too, but she never said anything and neither did Freddy. Freddy drank. A lot. Probably started when he was thirteen or younger. Smart kid, but what are you going to do when you have shitty role models?"

Dill stopped talking. Dad let the silence draw out for a while, then decided Dill needed a little prodding. "What kind of trouble did he get into with the law?"

"Look, Freddy is long past all of this. He got sober when he was twenty. I'm pretty sure he hasn't had a drink since."

"I wouldn't be digging around in his past if it wasn't necessary," Dad said.

"I know. I just hate the thought of all this coming back up. It's going to be hard on Freddy too, if he has to face it."

"Tell me," Dad said, making it clear that it was as much

an order as a request.

"Lots of minor stuff in his early teens, mostly to do with drinking. Some petty theft. He did some time in a few diversion programs for troubled kids, but nothing really took. You know the story. Anyway, when he was sixteen there was an incident out at Piney Knoll. You know how kids used to go out there and park by the pond. On this night, a girl got raped and beat up pretty bad. She and her boyfriend had gone out there for a bit of necking when they got into a fight. The boyfriend just drove off and left her there to find her own way home. She started to walk home when someone grabbed her from behind. She was dragged back to the pond and assaulted. There was only a sliver of moon that night, so she didn't get a good look at her attacker. Of course, she was traumatized by the whole event."

"How does Freddy fit into this?"

"Freddy regularly hung out at the pond drinking. Usually with his buddies, but he'd been known to go there by himself. In fact, another couple claimed to have seen him there about an hour before the attack. He was the first and best suspect. He was brought in, and keep in mind that this was back in the days when no one thought you could get a false confession from someone. They questioned him for a ludicrous amount of time. Who knows what techniques they used, but in the end, he confessed to the rape."

"He went to jail for it?"

"Almost. His parents didn't help him at all. In fact, his scumbag father told the paper that he always knew the kid was trouble. The only thing that saved Freddy was some semen left on the girl's pants. The culprit had worn a condom, but apparently when he took it off, some of the semen got on her pants leg. The stain wasn't noticed at first.

"Freddy got lucky with a good public defender. This was before DNA testing was a common thing, but it turned out that the attacker was a secretor, so they could tell that his blood type was B-positive and Freddy's is A. The prosecutor and the sheriff at the time didn't want to let it go, so they tried to claim that all it meant was that there had been another attacker present. But the girl wouldn't go along with it. She was adamant there had only been one person.

"In the end, Freddy walked free. But if he was messed up before, he was really a handful afterward. Any time he came into contact with law enforcement, it was a struggle. I approached him once for public intoxication, and even knowing me, he still fought me. I could have written him up for resisting with violence. But... I knew his history."

"So how'd he get clean?" I asked. I couldn't believe that this was the life story of the good-natured man I'd known for years.

"Judge Howard. He was the one that forced them to dismiss the rape case against Freddy, so he knew what had been done to him. I guess Freddy was about twenty when he came before the judge for something. I don't remember the specifics. Judge Howard kind of took Freddy under his wing. He got the county to pay for a rehab program and then he helped him get the job with the county after he finished the program."

"Judge Howard was that kind of guy," Dad said.

"I saw Freddy at his funeral about a decade later, bawling his eyes out. I think Freddy had finally found a father-figure that he could count on."

"Thanks, Dill. You can go back to sleep now."

"Nah. I'll get up and sit with Glenda. She hates storms. Been sitting in the living room all night with a flashlight waiting for a limb to come crashing through the roof."

"You can put this phone call on the clock."

"Really?"

"No," Dad said and hung up.

CHAPTER EIGHTEEN

"I guess Freddy has some understandable PTSD when it comes to being questioned by law enforcement," I said.

"You never know what other people have gone through."

"Do you think this is something that might have given Klein leverage over Freddy?"

"Maybe. Though there are any number of people who already know about Freddy's history. It only took me one phone call. The rape story would have been big news back in the day, so it doesn't really strike me as prime blackmail material," Dad said thoughtfully.

"Unless there's more to the story. Maybe Freddy really *was* involved with the attack and there was someone else there that night who saw it. If Klein got information from that third party saying Freddy actually was guilty, that would have the potential to undermine everything Freddy has built over the years. That would certainly be worth protecting," I suggested.

"Agreed. I know Freddy better than you. Let me talk with him and see if he'll agree to answer a few questions."

Dad left and I looked at my watch. It was two in the morning and the storm was still raging. The adrenaline that had driven me during the search for Cara had long faded and

I was exhausted. I knew that I really should go next door and talk to Charley, but I didn't want to go back out into the rain. *I'll call him in a few minutes*, I thought, then went to check on Cara again. It was a silly thing to do—she certainly wasn't going back outside and there were plenty of people willing to keep an eye on her. But I needed to see her to assure myself she was really there.

Cara seemed relaxed, chatting with Melvina while she cupped a mug of something warm in her hands.

"You're looking better," I told her.

"So I was looking bad before?" Cara said, and I admired her ability to still make a joke after what had been an insane experience.

"There aren't many women who would look real good after being wrapped up like a mummy and left out in a hurricane. Even so, you did it with grace and dignity," I said, and got a smile from both women.

"Suck up," Melvina said to me. "If you're going to be here for a few minutes, I'm going to the john."

"Had any luck figuring out what's behind this?" Cara asked when we were alone.

"Not that you'd notice. We've talked to most of the people who were unaccounted for when you were attacked. Nothing points toward any one person."

"I'm sorry I can't remember anything." Cara looked down at her mug.

I took her hand. "Don't beat yourself up over that. Anyone who went through what you did would be in the same situation. You got a pretty good whomp on the head. I agree with Dr. Patrick, though. I'll feel better once we've gotten you to the hospital for X-rays."

She looked up at me and smiled. "Did you just say I should have my head examined?"

"Now that you mention it, you probably should have done it as soon as you decided that hanging out with me was a good idea."

"It was the best idea I've had in a long time," she said

and squeezed my hand.

"Do you forgive me for not telling you about Klein and the camera in our room?"

"You'd have to do something pretty bad for me not to forgive you. I'll admit, I was going to hold that one over you a little longer, but after tonight..." She smiled.

Lucky, lucky man, I thought. Unbidden, my mind pulled up the nightmare vision of what my life would be like if I had lost her for good. I wrapped my arms around her and thought, *I need to make sure I never lose her.*

Melvina came back from her trip to the bathroom and I kissed Cara on the top of her head. "I need to check on Charley," I told her and headed for a quiet corner to make a phone call.

As I walked across the room, I noticed that a number of people were taking naps in whatever uncomfortable positions they could find on the floor or in chairs. It would be a busy day for everyone once dawn broke and Marcy moved on. Just assessing the amount of damage would take time, not to mention the clean-up.

I saw Dad sitting next to Freddy. Both men were leaning back in their chairs, looking relaxed. He seemed to be getting somewhere with Freddy and it would be good to be able to clear him.

Thinking about Dad, I suddenly felt guilty. He should have been getting some rest while he had the chance, instead of dealing with this. Whatever *this* was. A murder? Two murders? Two murders, an assault and an abduction? I sighed and dialed Charley.

"I'm fine. It's been quiet except for that old crepe myrtle on the east side of the building banging up against the boards on the window. Scared the hell out of me the first time I walked by it. Have you had any luck finding whoever's behind the attacks?" Charley asked.

"Not yet. Keep your eyes and ears open over there."

"Will do."

"We're working on a timeline that will cover everyone at

both facilities. We'll need to sit down with you at some point."

"Sure, anytime," he said, sounding unconcerned.

"Call if you need anything," I said, seeing Dad stand up and wave at me.

"Don't worry, I won't play the hero," Charley assured me and hung up.

"Freddy's going to talk with us," Dad said when I joined them.

Once we were in Bevin's office, Freddy looked tense as Dad told him about the recording and what our goals were for the interview. "I want to apologize for the way I reacted earlier," he said to me before we could ask any questions.

"It's okay. I've had some conversations that made yours look like only a three out of ten on the overreaction scale," I said, being completely honest.

"When I canvassed the room earlier in the evening, you weren't real sure where you'd been when Cara was abducted, and no one else I talked to could tell me either," Dad said, opening the door for Freddy to give a quick explanation.

"Yeah, I know," Freddy said, looking down at his feet.

Dad gave him a minute, then said, "Now that you've had some time to think about it, can you tell us where you were?"

"I was outside," Freddy finally said.

"In the storm?"

"If you go out the back, there's a small alcove that's protected from the weather. The wind was coming from the east, so it was fairly dry even with the storm."

"How'd you get to that side of the building?"

"I went out the door in the hallway by the bathrooms," he said, and I tried to envision the door.

"Isn't that door an emergency exit?" I asked.

"With an alarm," Dad added.

Freddy gave us a look that implied we were idiots, then explained, "I'm a supervisor in public works. I've also supervised maintenance crews for most of the county-owned buildings. I know every part of these buildings and can open almost any door. That includes being able to disable the alarm on an emergency exit."

Dad's eyebrows were raised. "Remind me to put you on the security assessment team the next time we're doing an evaluation of county buildings," he said.

"I could point out a few loopholes, for sure," Freddy said. He looked relaxed for the first time since we'd started talking.

"So we know how you got out there. What were you doing?"

Freddy looked shy... or maybe embarrassed. Eventually, he said, "I'm not a fan of being locked in a building. That was part of it. I kind of felt closed in with the storm and being inside with everyone." He hesitated, took a deep breath and went on. "It's mighty close to the jail. I could smell the place... I just wanted to get out for a minute."

"Did you see anyone or did anyone see you?" I asked him.

"I don't know. I think there was someone coming out of the bathroom when I went out, but I just heard the door open. I didn't see anyone." There was another pause before he added, "I made a phone call out there."

We waited, thinking he would elaborate. Nothing. Why was he being so coy?

"You know we're going to ask who you called," Dad said.

"Yeah, I know. I shouldn't be embarrassed. I've been working on it. After all these years, you'd think I'd be proud. I think talking about my sobriety just reminds me of when I wasn't sober. I was talking to a guy I sponsor. I found out that talking to someone I sponsor helps me more than talking to my own sponsor. Go figure."

Is everyone around here in AA? I wondered. I seemed to interact with more than my share of recovering addicts.

"We'll need to talk to him," I said, knowing what was coming next.

"There's an anonymity code," Freddy said. "But I don't

think he'll mind giving you a call. I'll talk to him and ask him to call you."

Not optimal, but at this point there weren't a lot of options.

"Can I see your phone?" I asked.

Freddy pulled it out and handed it to me. "I know you can look at the number and do a reverse lookup, but I'd appreciate you not doing that, and giving me a chance to have him call you instead."

"Sure," I said, a little unhappily, though the times on his phone checked out. I did make a mental note of the number before handing it back.

"What do you think?" I asked Dad after we let Freddy go

"None of them stand out one way or the other. You need to dive deeper into everyone's background. There has to be a connection. These aren't just a random series of senseless crimes."

"It has to be Blake Klein. He's the only connection we've found between the victims and criminals. He has to be blackmailing someone."

"I was on the boat and saw the same crash you did. If I had thought for one minute Klein could have survived that, I would have been willing to contribute all of my time to finding him over the last couple of months."

"I know." I couldn't see what I couldn't see. Something was missing from the equation, but I had no idea what it was. "I'm going to check in with Darlene," I said, and Dad left me to it.

"You don't think I need any sleep?" was how she answered the phone this time.

"You're the one that shows up at the office two hours early," I reminded her.

"That's a little different than spending a whole night without sleep. Now, when I was younger…"

"You're just hanging out at the hospital with your boyfriend anyway."

"Did you know he snores? Though, thanks to him, we

did score a couple of couches in somebody's office."

"You just lost all my sympathy. Did you have a chance to dig up any more information? Anything on Charley Wright?"

"Are you focusing in on him?"

"Who knows? I'm doing the scattershot routine. He's just on my mind right now."

"Nothing much. He worked down in Panama City at a construction firm for a while. He was one of their engineers. He took about a month break before moving up here. I got most of this from his employment application for his present job. I was able to tap into Major Parks's notes from the interview. He asked why Charley wanted to take a self-imposed demotion to maintenance worker. The major was convinced by Charley's explanation of wanting a simpler life after a divorce, etc. When I read it, though, the explanation didn't ring as true to me."

"You think he was lying?"

"Hiding something."

"I want to check the security camera footage for the sheriff's office again," I said with a determination born of sleep depravation.

"You sound like you could use a nap," Darlene said. "Shame you don't have these nice comfy couches."

"We have cots," I said, remembering how uncomfortable they were. Most of the people in the center were choosing to sleep in a chair rather than commit to one of the cots that looked like military castoffs.

"You might want to use one, sport," she said and hung up.

I found Dad and convinced him to return to Bevin's office once again. He was able to log-in and access the feed from the cameras over at the sheriff's office.

"Why is that one out?" I asked, pointing to one camera angle that was noticeably black.

"That's the one on the back door. It's been out for a week. Lionel looked at it and ordered a part, but you know how that is. Could be a couple weeks before it comes in."

"So we don't have any cameras on the back door?"

"No, but we do have the key access data," Dad said, but something about that bothered me. "And we have all the other cameras in back."

"But Charley could have gotten out through that door unnoticed if he'd wanted to?" I said, voicing the question as much to myself as to Dad. I was remembering our interview with Freddy.

"I suppose. Good point. Let's look at footage during the time that Cara went missing."

He pulled up several images from inside the building and rewound them until the timestamps were at the beginning of our timeframe. Playing them forward, we were able to keep track of Charley. While there were plenty of areas within the office that weren't covered by the cameras, there was enough footage of Charley to know that he couldn't have attacked Cara.

"What about the attack on Luke?"

"We looked at that footage. The man in the mask entered through the front after painting the cameras there," Dad reminded me, sounding tired.

"I want to see what Charley was doing," I urged.

With a sigh, he rewound the footage and hunted for the timestamps on all the cameras.

"Go to the time about ten minutes before the intruder shows up on the front camera," I said and Dad obliged.

"There. Charley is going into the break room. He gets a drink and sits down in the corner under the camera."

"He moves out of view," I corrected him. "We don't know if he sits down or not. The camera in the break room doesn't cover the door. Just the machines."

"That's because some hooligan was vandalizing the machines to get chips or some crap a few months ago," Dad said, shaking his head.

"The break room is near the back door. It's possible he could have gotten out that door without being seen," I said, and Dad sat up a little straighter and leaned closer to the screen. "Pull up all the working cameras that face the back of the building."

We watched the external video for the time after Charley went off-screen in the break room.

"You can't see enough of the building without the camera on the back door," Dad said, frustrated. "He could easily slide around the side of the building."

"Wait, rewind," I said. My eyes had seen something, but my mind didn't know what.

"That camera," I said, pointing to the image from the camera on the left of the building. "Let it move forward. There! Go back and do it in slow motion this time."

He did and for the third time I saw a flash of light. "Did you see that?"

"Lightning?"

"Check the same footage on the other camera," I said. He did and there was no flash. "One more time on the other camera."

When he did, I saw him smile. "That's the door opening."

We were seeing the light from inside illuminating the rain.

Dad started to pull up another program. "He would have had to use his keycard," he said, but before I could say anything, I saw him deflate. "Damn it! We just heard that Freddy was able to bypass the alarm on the door in this building."

"Exactly. With a little bit of thought, time and effort, I'm sure Charley could figure out a way to bypass the security pad on the back door. I know that he's worked with Lionel to fix it sometimes."

"But he wasn't involved in Cara's abduction," Dad said, trying to see what we were missing.

"Unless he could rig the footage or... he has an accomplice," I said.

"Or, like some of the other people we've interviewed tonight, he had some stupid reason of his own for sneaking out of the building."

"True. But we need to find out. I'm going over to talk with him," I said.

"You want me to go along?"

"No, but if you haven't heard back from me in half an hour, send the cavalry."

Once more, I grabbed a raincoat and flashlight to head out into the deluge. The eye of the storm had passed to the west of us more than an hour ago, but the winds in the tail of the storm were still fierce. As I opened the door, I had a moment when I thought I should reconsider Dad's offer to accompany me, but I shook myself and stepped out into the tempest again.

Now that I thought we might have caught the tail of the tiger, I tried to figure out the rest of the puzzle. Motive. Not just for the crimes, but for the threats. That's what the email to Luke and the card found on Hutton had been. Even more so, the attack on Cara. Who had those been aimed at? Me. But why? Dad had been as instrumental as I was in bringing Blake Klein down. Why not target him as well? Klein could have had all kinds of fun screwing Dad politically from afar.

What had all of this accomplished? Why had it come to a head tonight? All I was supposed to be doing that night was watching over the evidence room. Suddenly, like finding the key to a cypher, that one thought answered a dozen questions.

I was supposed to be guarding the evidence room and someone wanted me away from it. On the same night that a hurricane was plowing across the county. The one night when a criminal might have a chance to tamper with a room that held drugs and money valued at more than some banks kept in their vaults, but that wasn't nearly as secure as a bank vault.

I was walking faster now. I dropped my right hand and felt the reassuring presence of my Glock at my side. At the back door, I hesitated for only a moment. *I'll have surprise on my side*, I thought and used my card on the keypad. With the rain still pouring down, it took me two tries and some muttered curses to get it to work. Then I opened the door and stepped out of the rain.

As soon as I was inside, I realized I'd been completely wrong about who had the advantage of surprise. Standing in front of me, holding his own gun, was Dr. Greg Patrick. Oddly, he was wearing a small light strapped to his head.

"We meet again. How's that? Or maybe I should say, 'Dr. Livingston, I presume.' Or some other clever quip. Doesn't really matter. This time we've disconnected all of the cameras, so none of it will be preserved for posterity."

"You're in this with Charley," I said, watching him carefully to see how steady his gun hand was. Pretty damn steady.

"I would say that he was in it with me. But that's just quibbling," Dr. Patrick said.

"Whatever you're after, you won't get it," I said, letting my arm feel where my gun rested while thinking through the moves that would be required to get it in my hand and pointed in the right direction. But Dr. Patrick was wise to me.

"Put your hands up. Don't even think about going for your gun," he said, then added, "Doctor's orders."

I was still holding my keycard and my flashlight. I started to put the keycard into my pocket, but he said, "Just drop the card. And the flashlight too." Down they both went.

"Does Blake Klein really have anything to do with this?" I asked.

"Oh, yeah. He's the man pulling the strings."

"Bullshit!"

"Let's just say his name came up at a planning meeting. Look, I'd love to talk about all of this, but there's work to be done. This hurricane isn't going to hang around forever. I really should go ahead and shoot you." He seemed to think about it for a moment. "But not yet. If we need a hostage, you'll be available. Take out your cell phone. Carefully."

I did what he said, hoping for an opening.

"Drop the phone on the floor and stomp on it."

"I could just take the battery out," I tried to joke.

"Smash the phone," he ordered, and I did. "Now turn around and face the wall. Legs spread, hands as high as they'll go."

"You sound like you've been on the other end of the orders," I said.

"Just do it. It's been kind of fun playing cops and robbers with you, but we really need to get this over with."

"Where's your partner?"

"Shut up and turn around now, or I'll forget the hostage option," he said, putting me firmly in the sights of his Beretta.

I turned and put my hands against the wall. He came over and pushed the gun hard against my spine, sending me a clear message. Then he tried to pull my gun out of its holster and couldn't.

"What the hell?" he growled, his voice full of frustration and anger. The barrel against my back pushed in harder.

"It's a retention holster. You have to press the little plastic tab on the side as you draw the gun. I can show you," I offered.

"Keep your hands on the wall."

He struggled with my gun for another few seconds. If his gun hadn't been inches from my spine, I would have had an opportunity to make a move. But I wasn't stupid enough to try it and he eventually got my gun. He stepped away from me, emptying the chamber and throwing the magazine to the side, then he stuck the gun in his waistband

Suddenly, there was a tremendous noise and the whole building shook. I assumed a tree had fallen against it. Then the lights went out, the only illumination coming from the glowing red emergency exit signs.

The doctor's attention wavered just enough for me to throw myself at him. I didn't have any choice really. I couldn't go out the door I came in without my keycard, and the break room was a dead end. But I wasn't close enough to properly tackle him, and instead grabbed him by his legs and knocked him off balance.

Unfortunately, he held onto his gun. In the position I was in, I wouldn't have a chance in a struggle over the weapon, so I did the only thing I could think of. I scrambled away over the top of him. I got to my feet, slipping and sliding on the tile floor as I tried to get my balance. I heard a shot ring out behind me, but the bullet went wild and hit the wall.

I made it around the corner and my mind started searching for a way to turn the tables. A gun was my first thought, but every gun in the office was under lock and key and I didn't have any of the keys. I couldn't even get out of the building. I could hear Dr. Patrick stalking toward me, but there were also some very odd, loud sounds coming from Shantel's office.

Curiosity will be the death of me. I turned toward Shantel's office, then saw a fire alarm in the glow from the emergency lights. On my way past, I pulled the alarm and heard only a few weak reports through the building. Whatever had happened to the lights had also affected the fire alarm system.

Racing down the hallway toward Shantel's office, I could see strange lights and movement through the glass window in the door. The noise from the room was beginning to drown out the storm. I just had time to think about the fact that I didn't have a key to the room, when that problem solved itself. The door, along with part of the ceiling and the wall, crumbled before my eyes as I slid to a stop. The destruction knocked out the emergency lighting above the door and the hallway was plunged into almost total darkness.

With the roar of machinery competing with the wind and rain that was now inside the building, I stood there and stared for a moment. There was enough light from the machine's headlights for me to figure out that someone, probably Charley, had used the bucket excavator from the construction site to smash into Shantel's office. That's when I caught a flash of light from behind me. Stupidly, I turned to see what was coming. It was Dr. Patrick, wearing his headlamp. There was another gunshot and I heard the bullet whiz past me. When you have only one choice, making a decision isn't that hard. I turned and stumbled through the rubble into the evidence room.

I crawled over the door, where I was caught in the headlights of the excavator. The behemoth paused for a moment, before roaring back to life and charging at me. This was actually good fortune disguised as a moment of terror. The excavator's attack knocked more of the ceiling down, which pushed Dr. Patrick backward and off his feet.

Again my options were limited. I knew that Dr. Patrick had a gun, but I also assumed that the excavator would be less likely to crush me to death if there was a chance of hitting Dr. Patrick in the process, so I ran clumsily over debris toward the doctor. Whoever was driving the excavator was trying to knock me down with the bucket, which swung past me twice. I managed to jump on Dr. Patrick who, thankfully, had managed to lose the Beretta in the jumble of ceiling tiles, concrete blocks and office furniture that filled the half demolished room.

Lying on top of Dr. Patrick, I managed to pin both of his hands down. Behind me, I could hear the engine of the excavator revving as though the driver was trying to decide whether to just go ahead and crush both of us. I felt the bucket swing past my head again, forcing me to lie as flat as I could against Dr. Patrick, who was bucking and struggling to free himself. He outweighed me and was in good shape, so all I could do was ride him like a bronco amid the destruction, rain and wind, while trying to keep from having my head knocked off by the huge metal bucket swinging through the air.

The stalemate seemed to drag on forever when I suddenly felt hands around my arms, pulling me back. I flailed at them and that's when I heard Dad's voice in my ear. "You got him. We're here now!" he said, screaming to be heard over the sounds of the storm and the angry machine.

I looked down at Dr. Patrick and an image of him with his hands on Cara rose before my eyes. Dad hadn't managed to pull us completely apart yet and, with one savage motion, I slammed my forehead into his face. It would be hours before I felt the pain from the blow. At that moment, I was filled with the joy of getting a little bit of revenge.

Dad yanked me off the doctor at that point, saying, "That's enough, tiger."

Jerry Franks dropped a heavy knee on the doctor's chest in order to handcuff him. I fought to get my breath back and shook off Dad's grip. I watched Dad start to step around Dr. Patrick, but then one of his big boots came down hard on the doctor's ankle. I was sure it was just an accident.

CHAPTER NINETEEN

An hour later, I was sitting in the emergency management center next to Cara. I'd gotten a shower and was drinking hot tea while dressed in clothes borrowed from another deputy at the jail.

"Aren't we the pair?" Cara laughed.

"You rock the deputy look better than I do," I said with a wink.

"They did all of this just to rob the evidence room?" she said in disbelief.

"There's several million dollars' worth of drugs in there, and another two hundred thousand in cash and jewelry. Add on to that, about fifty or more guns. It was worth it to them. We'll have to see what we dig up, but Charley, the doctor and Hutton were all in the same area west of here a couple years ago. I'll be surprised if we don't find some evidence tying them all together. We'll be spending some time plowing through their histories once the storm is over and things get back to normal. Which reminds me, what's the latest on the storm?"

"The worst should be over," she said, taking my hand and clutching it in hers, and I knew she wasn't just talking about the hurricane.

At dawn, Cara and I walked over and looked at the destruction of the sheriff's office. Dad was helping half a dozen deputies secure tarps over everything they could. A light rain was still falling and the wind kept whipping the blue tarps around, making it difficult to tie them down.

"At least you stopped them before they completely destroyed the vault where most of the evidence is stored. It was breached, but we patched it up first and I've got one deputy inside. Besides the theft, we would have had to tell the State Attorney that a whole lot of cases had had their evidence lost or compromised," Dad said.

"What brought you to the rescue?" I asked him.

"The fire department called me and said they'd gotten an alarm from the office. They weren't going to respond because of the storm, but they felt they needed to let me know. Once I heard that, things started to fall into place."

Later that morning, I was finally able to drive Cara to the hospital in Tallahassee to be properly looked over. I only teased her a little about this reversal of our usual roles. Once she'd been seen by the doctor and was sent down for X-rays and scans, I hunted up Darlene and visited Luke.

I was surprised to see Mr. and Mrs. Lynch outside the ICU.

"We should have more answers for you soon," I told them.

"I'm not sure it was worth it," Martin said, looking over to where Luke lay in bed with his head wrapped and any number of tubes and wires connecting him to various machines.

"The prognosis is good," I said. "Luke wanted to help."

"We're going to stand by him. It's the least we can do. Make sure he gets what he needs," Martin said while Lori Lynch watched Luke through the glass.

Darlene and I were allowed to go in for a couple of minutes and give Luke the CliffsNotes version of what happened. His eyes grew large and a small smile appeared on his face.

"It's going to make a nice epilogue to your true crime book on Blake Klein," I told him.

When he tried to nod, he winced and I saw him hit his morphine button.

Once Cara was given a clean bill of health, we drove home to see if our house had survived the storm. There were a lot of trees down along the way, but no major obstacles on the roads or our driveway. As soon as we were in sight of the house, I could tell that something was wrong. It just didn't look right. When we got closer, I could see that half of one of the ancient oaks in the yard had fallen toward the house.

Holding my breath, I got out of the car to see how much damage it had done to the house. I was more than relieved to see that, other than a few missing shingles and some crumpled siding, the house was intact.

"When we pick up Alvin and Ivy, I need to grab Dad's big chainsaw," I told Cara.

The plan had been to get the animals and go back home, but when we got to Dad's there were a couple of trees down in his yard, including one that had crushed part of the pasture fence. Luckily, Finn and Mac were oblivious to the damage, happily grazing in their soggy pasture. As Dad was still tied up at the office for God knew how long, I spent the rest of the evening helping Jamie cut up the tree and patch the fence.

When we finished, we found that Genie had prepared a huge pot of chili that tasted amazing. Later, I managed to wrestle Ivy back into her carrier and Cara got Alvin to his feet for the trip to the car.

"He and Alvin were up all night," Jamie said when I went over to pet Mauser, who was sprawled on the floor. He lifted his head a bit before dropping it heavily back to the floor.

"I appreciate you looking after everyone," I told him, ruffling his ears. He huffed in acknowledgment. "And also for showing me how to do a professional head-butt."

"See, it was just a bunch of wind and rain," Jimmy, Genie's son, proclaimed when he walked us out to the car.

Three days later, the office was back on a normal schedule. Power had been restored to about half the county, though it was still expected to be a day or two before it would be back on at our property. I was sitting in the conference room with Pete and Darlene as we put the various pieces together to send over to the State Attorney. Charley Wright had clamped his mouth shut and refused to say anything, but luckily Dr. Patrick's ego wouldn't let him keep quiet about his plan and all the work he'd put into it.

"Dr. Patrick, Hutton and Charley all met at the North Florida Correctional facility. Patrick was the prison's doctor. Hutton was incarcerated and Charley was working on an expansion of the main building. They got together to deal drugs originally, and did some of that down on the coast, including on Pelican Island. But all three are adamant that they never met Blake Klein," Darlene said. She'd spent most of the nights since the storm at Hondo's apartment in Tallahassee, which had miraculously been able to restore most of its power by evening of the first day.

"Which came first, the chicken or the egg?" Pete asked.

"Let me see if I can get this straight," I said. "Darlene, correct me if I get off track. Originally, Charley had gotten out of construction to get away from drugs. This was after meeting Patrick and Hutton and helping them out on the coast. He got a job with us and was, apparently, trying to go straight. Then Hutton and Patrick heard about the Thompson clan getting nailed. With the elimination of a major dealer in the area, they got the idea they could come in here and take over. It was a huge bonus that they had Charley on the inside of the biggest law enforcement agency in the area. When Charley learned about the plans for the addition, he started speculating about how they could use construction equipment to smash into the evidence room and make off with all the drugs and cash."

"He must have become disillusioned with the straight

life," Darlene said wryly.

"Exactly," I said. "Once they realized that a hurricane was headed this way, they fast-tracked their plain."

"So whose idea was it to use Klein?" Pete asked.

Darlene took over the narrative. "Before the hurricane gave them a golden opportunity, the original plan had been to distract you and your dad with the idea that Blake Klein was back. Turns out it was the nepotism billboard that reminded Patrick of Luke's articles about Klein's crimes on Pelican Island and your involvement." She looked at me. "See, those signs have already had an affect."

"That doesn't make me feel any better."

"So why did they kill Lynch?" Pete asked.

"Sadly, that was a real suicide," Darlene said. "Being the assholes that they are, they just decided to use the opportunity to get the conspiracy theory rolling."

"And Hutton?"

"He was going a bit mad. Used too much of his own product and liked the armed robbery shtick way more than he should have," I said. "Dr. Patrick and Charley agreed to eliminate him and escalate things before the storm by leaving a card with Klein's name in his wallet. We're going to have some work to do to prove which of them actually pulled the trigger. They're both pointing the finger at each other. Big surprise."

"Luke showing up here wasn't part of the plan. Turns out that Luke knew Dr. Patrick. He'd seen him a couple of times on Pelican Island when Patrick was working the party scene down there. Patrick was the one who decided Luke had to go."

"And they almost succeeded," I said, thinking about Luke. He'd still looked like hell when the Lynches had wheeled him out of the hospital the day before.

"Now the abduction of Cara *was* part of the plan," Darlene said. "They figured it was the perfect way to manipulate Larry and give Charley time alone in the building. If Larry was hanging around the office too much, they were going to keep sending clues that Cara was here or there and have him and any other deputies nearby off chasing their tails."

"Would have worked too, except you all found her before they wanted her to be found," Pete said, clapping me on the back.

Someone else was a little harder on me about the whole thing.

"One job. You had just one job," Shantel said, shaking her head as she helped me with the evidence list. This was about the hundredth time I'd heard this since Shantel had first seen that her office had been ripped open. The excavator's bucket had even come down squarely on top of her desk at one point during the fight.

"It was a giant, menacing hunk of machinery. I did what I could," I joked.

She gave me the squint-eye as the blue tarps flapped overhead. "I guess I'll get a whole bunch of new equipment out of it," she huffed. "By the way, I got Charley's left thumb print off of one of the batteries that came out of the game camera you found on your property. I can't believe that man. Worked with him for two years. And I'd liked him too." Shantel shook her head.

After work, I picked Cara up from the vet and we drove to Dad's where we'd been cleaning up every night before heading home to our dark house. While I was waiting for Cara to finish her shower, my phone rang.

"Did you give Baggie's mom my phone number?" Eddie asked.

"No. We might have talked about you, but I never gave her your number."

"She wants me to get Baggie clean. Now how the hell am I going to do that?"

"Maybe it's Karma. You and Mr. Griffin came through the storm pretty well. What'd you say, just lost a few roof tiles? Plus you got your lights on in two days."

"What's that got to do with Baggie?" Eddie asked,

sounding suspicious.

"I'm just saying if you have some good luck, you should pass it on. Helping Baggie get clean can be your way of thanking your higher power for all that he, she or they have done for you," I said.

There was a long silence on the other end of the line. Finally, he said, "If I get Baggie clean, I might be owed a little more good fortune."

"Karma. Go get it, my friend," I told him.

When Cara and I got home, I flipped the light switch just out of habit, not expecting anything to happen. Amazingly, there was light.

"Electricity shouldn't make me so happy," Cara said.

"Your hippy parents would be disappointed," I told her. "Actually, *I'm* a little disappointed. I'd planned on dinner by candlelight."

"No, you didn't," she said, hitting me lightly on the arm

"Yes, I really did."

"There's a switch."

I went out to the car and came back in with a huge cooler stuffed with food.

"Where did you get all this?" she said, her eyes wide.

"Sarah has been cooking for everyone. Pete says she feels guilty because of the generator. They've had electricity the whole time. Pete brought all of this to me before I left work today."

"Wow, it looks great."

We set the table. There were still candles lying about, so I put a few on the table and lit them.

"For a change, the four-footed ones aren't bothering us," I said, looking over at Ivy and Alvin, who were both sleeping on the couch.

"They're still recovering from all the excitement of the storm and spending the night with Gigantadog," Cara laughed.

"Have you remembered anything else from that night?" I asked her gently.

"I'm not trying. If it comes back, I'll deal with it then," she said with a practicality I admired.

I turned the lights off before sitting down.

"Seriously, what's with all the romantic atmosphere?" Cara asked. The light of the candles flickered in her bright blue eyes.

Slowly, I pulled a small ring box out of my pocket, keeping it clutched in my hand. She looked at me.

"I thought this was fitting, but now I'm not so sure. You might think it's a bit strange. I... I just... That's when I realized I couldn't lose you."

I set the box on the table and Cara reached out to open it.

"I conned a friend from high school into working overtime at Market Jewelers. It's made from a piece of the chain I found on the car." Truth was, it hadn't been hard to convince my friend to do the work. He was more than happy for an excuse to spend long nights at the downtown store, where there had been power and running water.

She took the ring out of the box. My friend had used silver solder to bond the chain into a ring, then had topped it with a small diamond in a simple round setting.

"If you want, we can get another ring later."

"No. It's perfect. Just perfect," Cara said softly.

"There's also a new chain for your pendant."

"Are you trying to ask me something?" she said, slipping the ring on her left hand with a big smile.

"Yes, yes. Okay, I need a do-over." I took her hand. "Cara, will you marry me?"

"Let me think." She paused for a minute, but was unable to keep a straight face. "Yes, of course I will."

I leaned over the table to kiss her and almost lit myself on fire with one of the candles.

"Is this what life is going to be like with you? Happiness mixed with a little danger?" she asked, laughing as she made sure my shirt wasn't still burning.

"Oh, yeah," I said, and kissed her again. The storm had

passed and that night was one of the best of my life.

A week later, I got a phone call that proved the nightmare was really over. The storm had washed Blake Klein's skull up onto Pelican Island.

Larry Macklin returns in:

October's Fear
A Larry Macklin Mystery–Book 12
Coming Winter 2019

AFTERWORD

From the earliest days of the Larry Macklin Mysteries, it had always been my intention to set the September book during a hurricane. What I couldn't have anticipated was that, just a few short weeks after the original ebook publication of *September's Fury*, I would be in the middle of a storm more frightening than the one I had just written about.

It was October, not September, and it was named Michael, not Marcy. But in many other ways, including its rapid development and final path, Michael was eerily similar. Michael, however, was much stronger, slamming the Florida Panhandle just short of Category 5 strength and quickly taking its place in the record books next to other monsters such as Andrew, Camille and the Labor Day Hurricane of 1935.

It was the strongest storm ever to hit this part of Florida and it brought small towns from the coast to the Georgia border to their knees. Even as I write this, more than a month after the storm, hundreds of people are still living in tent cities or other temporary housing and the clean-up continues.

I'm the first to admit that I had a rather cavalier attitude about this storm. Much like a conversation Larry has with Cara in *September's Fury*, I truly believed the storm would lose power as soon as it hit the coast, and that my property was far enough inland to see no more than tropical storm-, or possibly Category 1-force, winds. I was very, very wrong.

I and my family were also very, very lucky. Miraculously, all things of value on the property made it through the storm unscathed. Our three horses and ten outdoor cats were all fine. Though I can easily count more than 100 downed trees in the front part of our property alone, the only significant damage was to fencing.

For the first few days, it was impossible to walk in a straight line anywhere on the property. It took us almost two days to clear our driveway and we were nine days without power and water. But many friends, relatives and neighbors stepped up to help us cut and move the worst of the trees so we could get water to our horses and begin to make some sense out of the chaos. And I was never so happy to see anyone in my life as the power crew who came to restore our lines and poles.

I'll never doubt the power of Mother Nature again. And I'll never forget how fortunate I was when so many others lost everything. If you are able to contribute to any of the support and recovery agencies doing work in the Florida Panhandle, please do. And consider a visit to our beaches, fishing towns and smaller communities in the future – they'll be back better and stronger and would appreciate the tourist dollars to help their economic recovery.

ACKNOWLEDGMENTS

The usual thanks go out to my wife, Melanie, for her editing skills and support; and to H. Y. Hanna for her inspiration, assistance and encouragement. And to all the fans of the series—thank you!!

Original Cover Concept by H. Y. Hanna
Cover Design by Robin Ludwig Design Inc.
www.gobookcoverdesign.com

ABOUT THE AUTHOR

A. E. Howe lives and writes on a farm in the wilds of north Florida with his wife, horses and more cats than he can count. He received a degree in English Education from the University of Georgia and is a produced screenwriter and playwright. His first published book was *Broken State*. The

Larry Macklin Mysteries is his first series and he released a new series, the Baron Blasko Mysteries, in summer 2018. The first book in the Macklin series, *November's Past*, was awarded two silver medals in the 2017 President's Book Awards, presented by the Florida Authors & Publishers Association; the ninth book, *July's Trials*, was awarded two silver medals in 2018. A member of the Mystery Writers of America, Howe is also the co-host of the "Guns of Hollywood" podcast, part of the Firearms Radio Network. When not writing or podcasting, Howe enjoys riding, competitive shooting and working on the farm.